ANNE KATIH

My King of Flowers

Honey Locust Books

2024

Honey Locust Books

For permissions requests, contact:
Email: honeylocustbooks@gmail.com
Website: http://honeylocustbooks.com

This book is a work of fiction. Names, characters, places, and incidents either are products of the author's imagination or are used fictitiously. Any resemblance to actual events or locales or persons, living or dead, is entirely coincidental.

First Edition, August 2024
ISBN: 9798227896858

To my king of flowers.

CONTENTS

A desperate wish, made from the heart, is always answered. Sooner or later.

My King of Flowers

A fragrance of peonies, so gentle and sweet, hung in the warm spring air around her, reminding her of her youth and the fleeting memories brought with them. Yinuo rushed through the streets, holding a hood by one hand to cover her head as the other gripped the package closest to her side. She ran to the alleyways for cover before shooting through two open-air restaurants.

"Jiějiě[1]!" her brother called for her, but she couldn't be caught! Not now, not when she was so close to home, and she didn't want her father to know she'd left the house without permission. Her brother's shadow gained on her, causing Yinuo to take a reckless turn into a dead end. She dropped her hood, clutching the package more carefully and scouring for anything to help her. Someone had stacked crates and barrels at the end of the alley, and without thinking of her bad leg, she raced to them and lifted herself up and over the wall. She rolled over just in time to fall into a bed of brush. "Omph!"

Yinuo waited a moment, smiling as she looked at the blue sky and the large head of pink peony brought front and center—the heavy fragrance lulling her into nostalgia. She had friends who rushed down the lanes for peach and cherry blossoms, but the small petals were nothing in comparison to the softness of peonies. She loved the silken feel of their petals against her cheek, pushing her nose into the center and being enveloped by the intoxicating scent.

She pushed herself up from the plant, suddenly remembering her package, franticly searching before finding the tightly bound silk fabrics. "Please, don't be broken...please," Yinuo whispered. Gingerly, she unraveled

---

[1] "big sister"

the layers, inhaling sharply when she reached the last one. A small jade figure of mandarin ducks revealed itself unharmed, and she breathed a sigh of relief. Her gift to her future sister-in-law remained intact, the lovely jade carved so preciously with details even in the feathers. She carefully wrapped it again and then looked around where she had landed.

Large leafy peony bushes encircled her, boasting heads in a spectrum of pink hues, each at various stages of bloom. The tranquility of the garden, which she had unexpectedly invaded, was absolute, with no cries of her name from her brother nearby. Sun shafts beamed through the redbud tree, its violet petals a burst of color over the full trunk and limbs of the specimen. Yet, even caught in the beauty of nature, she found herself staring at a man dozing in a wheelchair, his hand propped thoughtfully against his cheek. Yinuo heard his soft breaths, observed the subtle rise and fall of his chest, and was entranced by the man before her.

Frozen in place, her heart thrummed with each passing second. The man was clad in fine silks of white and blues, adorned with delicate clouds and phoenix embroidery on his outer robe. The long pao[2] pressed immaculately, layered sheer and satin blues beneath it. Her gaze traced the contour of his jawline, sharply defined yet softened by his long,

---

[2] Traditional loose-fitting robe with wide sleeves.

ebony hair, and descended towards his full, soft lips. His hand, pressed against the side of his face, inadvertently drew attention to the large scar that traversed the left side, beginning at his brow, slashing across his dark, deep-set eyes, and ending at his upper cheek. A smaller scar touched his chin.

Yinuo realized she had not yet been detected. She took an involuntary step back, rustling the leaves underfoot and sending the magpies scattering from the redbud tree. *No, it couldn't be him*, she thought bitterly. The disruption broke her reverie, and memories flooded back—Dehai, her childhood friend offering her a peony, her king of flowers. The man's eyes, a blue so vibrant they seemed to embody the essence of water, lifted to meet hers, bearing an unassuming expression. She was struck by a resemblance so poignant that for a fleeting moment she entertained the possibility, only for reality to jarringly reclaim her. *Dehai is dead.*

10 years prior...

Lord Yan's fourth son decided to surprise the fortune tellers and sour three of his aunts' fortunes by being born female. Although not what was desired, the elders welcomed Yinuo into their family as the only daughter. For all her milk years, Little Yinuo chased the dust of her brothers, mimicked their language, and nearly worried her mother into an early grave whenever she was brought back hurt. Yet, even with a scraped knee or bruised eye, the child often had a smile on her face, blissfully ignorant of anything being different.

Until she broke her leg. Sitting in the courtyard of her father's home, Yinuo was predominately displayed alongside her six brothers, kneeling in a row. Her leg had been wrapped in fracture powder, and she'd been given medicine and a chair for her comfort, but it did not excuse her from her father's discipline.

Sharing this punishment, she stole glances at each of her brothers. Weixin, the second son and future general, knelt firm and focused like he'd been since birth. The gentle and pragmatic nature of teaching her horseback riding was the furthest from his mind. Besides him, her brothers Danni and Ruijian shared black eyes—typical of their petty rivalry over the last mooncake. She'd never expected Mingdan, with his calloused scholar's hands, to ever think of bribing a classmate for access to the stables. And the youngest, Little Sile, still looked smug for sneaking away from old Nǎinai[3] to watch the races. This left Danbei, the eldest, who found himself unwittingly responsible for the actions of his siblings simply by virtue of his age.

---

[3] Grandma (paternal); also used respectfully for older women.

The boys shrunk in line as the physician passed with a disapproving glare. "This is your fault, mèimei[4]," Yan Danni, her third brother, grumbled.

"Shh!" Danbei chided, firming his stance and kneeling closest to Yinuo's chair.

"Father said nothing about speaking!" Yan Danni protested.

"We're lawn ornaments. Shut up, little brother," the fifth son, Ruijian, chided

"I'm older!"

"You whine enough!"

Their father merely glared out the window, and the boys shrunk in presence again. Despite the pain, Yinuo's world felt warm and genuine. She had her family by her side, and that made everything feel right. Father's horse had never seen such speed, and Yinuo had sent it into an epic trot before it launched her off that cliff. She'd do it again, feeling the wind against her face and the heartbeat of the horse at her legs. She smiled, remembering the feeling of freedom and excitement. Her youngest brother rolled his eyes.

"Jiějiě," he whispered on her left as he wobbled from knee to knee. "How are you feeling?"

"Fine," she smiled. Her brother cheated at the discipline by slightly leaning on her bamboo chair. When their father

---

[4] "little sister"

paced the window, he would straighten up and look like the others, a mini version of his five brothers. He'd been the one who dared her to race the horse faster and only suffered a scrape against his cheek when he fell chasing the horse. His eyes were bright and shined with vigor as he curled his arm around hers.

Their mother walked out of the house, heavily pregnant, followed by an entourage of maids and parasols. She strained her smile as she observed the line. "Sile, you're in the wrong order," she commented, "Go kneel by Mingdan on the end."

Sile obeyed, walking on his knees to the other side of the line of brothers. Their mother tapped the oldest two on the shoulder, allowing them to stand and rub out their knees. She turned to Yinuo with a scowl. "Carry your sister to the back gardens. Honestly, she is enough of a spectacle with her legs exposed."

"Is father feeling bad for us, yet, mother?" Danni glanced up with pleading eyes.

She returned it with a harsh scowl. "Not today, Danni. You have another hour, at least. Honestly..."

"Mother, you know raised words will upset your condition," Mingdan replied calmly, not even looking at her.

"You're not off the hook either! Trading tests! You're lucky the shifu doesn't expel you! Do you know how hard your father worked at his age!" She snapped at him.

Sile giggled, and Ruijian nudged him with his elbow, knowing better not to upset his mother's wrath. *Stop*, Ruijian warned him. Their mother sighed and then regained her composure and said, "Danbei, Weixin, pick up your sister. We're leaving." She marched them through to the back gardens, an inner section surrounded by peonies in near bloom. Yinuo groaned, but only for a moment, as Danbei gently placed her down at the center. They erected a tent above her to keep the sun partially off. Her mother sighed, "Good. Weixin and Danbei, go check on the horse now."

They bowed out, leaving Yinuo with a pleading look as they exited. For a moment, her mother let the silence pass between them, dismissing all but her most loyal maid. When they were out of ear shot she folded her arms and turned to her daughter. Yinuo could feel the calm before the storm, readying herself for another earful. She tried to dissuade her mother's anger. "Sit, Mother, you must be tired."

"If I sit, I'm not getting back up. I shouldn't be up now," she sighed.

"It really was an accident."

"You nearly lost your life for this. Yinuo, no more chasing your brothers. No more horseback riding, no more market visits, or leaving the house without permission."

"Mother!"

"I mean it, Yi'er[5]. You could have lost your life today. We don't even know if your leg will heal properly," she said. She sterned her expression and shook her head. "You are my only daughter. I expect you'll leave home one day, but I do not expect you to die on me. You're not allowed to."

"Mother, I didn't mean to worry you. Please stop crying."

Her mother wiped her face, flicking away the tears as if they were nothing. "This is for the best now. I'll have Maid Yaolin bring something for you to work on. A chore." Yinuo groaned, and her mother snapped, "Are you listening?"

"It's my leg!" she lied, covering her face and turning from her mother, who simply sighed and huffly exited the garden.

Time spent in the peony garden would be the most she had ever been apart from her brothers. While she still took her meals with her family, her life had turned from open fields and running with her brothers to a corner garden. She eventually settled into a routine of healing and diet changes, with Maid Yaolin supervising her brothers' visits. Sile visited first because he was the youngest and least likely to promote schemes. He snuck her candied tiger sugar sculptures and shared with her the secrets of beating Mingdan in Go. Though she appreciated her brother's enthusiasm, she

---

[5] "Yi'èr" – a term of affection used to shorten the name Yinuo to Yi'èr, similar to how "Emilie" might be shortened to "Emmy" in English.

fought down her tinge of jealousy. If only she hadn't broken her leg, she wouldn't be trapped in the garden.

"Shut up, dìdì[6]! Go away!" she shouted at him, catching herself as her lip trembled. She met the confused look of her little brother as if she had cut him with her words. She regretted it, biting her lip.

"What did I do?" his soft words struck her heart.

"N-Nothing... I just hurt. I can't play like I want; I'm trapped, and you're free. Go away! You remind me that I can't go outside anymore, nor will I ever learn to ride Father's horse."

"Jiějiě," he stuttered.

"Just leave!" she cried, but Sile didn't leave. Instead, he approached her and grabbed her arm, pulling it into an embrace.

"I'm not leaving, jiějiě. I'll never leave, jiějiě," he pouted.

"You fool," she said. He tilted his head and stuck out his tongue at her. "My jiějiě, no one else's..."

"What about Ruijian or Mingdan?" she asked.

"Mine," he said possessively. He brushed the tears from her face, "Okay, I can share because Mingdan makes you laugh, and Ruijian creates the best sculptures. I'll go get them, and you can beat Mingdan in Go[7]!" he said happily,

---

[6] "little brother"

[7] 1. Go (围棋, Wéiqí) – A board game involving two players who take turns placing black and white stones on a grid, aiming to capture the opponent's stones and control territory.

pushing off from his sister and rushing out of the garden. Yinuo watched him leave but knew he probably wouldn't return. Mingdan and Ruijian were both dedicated to their paths; Mingdan in his pursuit of knowledge, and Ruijian his future trade.

Maid Yaolin chased after her brother, leaving Yinuo completely alone in the garden. It was a crushing loneliness, hoping that someone, anyone, would be there.

"Dìdì!" she called, but no answer came. Yinuo shifted her weight from hip to hip to adjust herself in the chair. Her leg had been propped up by a stool, and the fracture powder itched at the center. She couldn't reach it, pushing her fingers between the bandages and trying her best to get access to the itch.

"What are you doing?" a man asked her; she looked up and saw the gardener and his son coming in with water buckets from the well. The man approached and placed the water down before bowing to her.

"My leg itches," she explained, still scratching at the top of her bindings.

The man pondered on it a moment, "En[8]. Dehai, keep her company. I will return shortly." The man left, and a boy around her age gave her a toothy grin. He shyly stepped

---

[8] Expression of agreement or acknowledgment.

back, holding his water bucket over his face. He couldn't have been a few years different than her. She studied him, canting her head to peer past the bucket.

"What are you doing?" she asked.

"N-Nothing, keeping you company," he stuttered his words.

"Do you have a name?"

He nodded.

"Then tell me what it is," she said happily, still trying to scratch the itch.

He shook his head quickly, raising the bucket again.

"I have six brothers. Think of me as a boy if you won't be so shy," she explained. Cautiously, the boy lowered his bucket, revealing his striking blue eyes, which stilled her entirely, even her previously racing hands, as she breathed in the moment. There was a depth to them, an unfathomable blue that sought her own, reminiscent of the boundless sky and stirring within her a sense of right she couldn't quite understand. This would be someone who made residency in her heart.

He shuddered, "D-Dehai."

"Dehai...Good. I'm Yinuo! You and I are going to be friends from now on."

"I-I don't know about that."

"I can feel it. Now, hand me that bucket!" she demanded.

"Why do you want my bucket?"

"I demanded it. Hand it over!" she boldly said. The boy looked to her and then back to the gate where his father had left him. He set down his bucket and shook his head.

"That doesn't sound like a good idea," he said. "I'll have to draw water from the well again, and I know what you're going to do."

"Really, hand over the bucket and see!" she prompted, smiling as she did. Despite her bravado, the boy stood several feet away from her, and no matter her screaming or demands, he didn't have to follow her orders. She was a child, and he wasn't going to upset his father.

He shook his head. "No, you're going to do something stupid!" he rebuked her.

Yinuo froze; she'd never been told "no" by a servant before; canting her head, she looked at him in awe. "Why can't I have the bucket? It'll help me."

"You're going to try and take off your bandages. The physician said that you shouldn't get it wet, and my father was warned about protecting your bindings. If we get it wet, we'll be whipped. So no, you can't have my bucket."

"...You look shy, but you can be pretty bold, servant," she mused.

"It's to protect your leg. The adults are worried about it."

"Really, what have they said?" she asked, folding her arms.

"They say you won't walk right again."

"Ha! I'm not only going to walk again. I am going to run! And then I'm going to beat up anyone who says that again! You first!"

"Ah, don't hit me."

"How can I hit you! I'm stuck to this chair! Idiot!"

Dehai circled around to her other side. He grabbed a large stalk of a peony without a head and carefully came to her side. Slowly, he approached her, keeping as much distance away from her as he possibly could, but extending the stalk. "Use this...for the itch."

Yinuo took the stalk and squeezed it between her bindings, finally able to scratch the side of her thigh. Relief swept through her with a moan as she smiled at Dehai. "Dehai! You're brilliant! I could hug you if I could reach you!"

"T-the sentiment is appreciated," he said, turning a bright shade of fuchsia. His father returned then, his expression thoughtful and intense. He was a man in his middle years, with neatly styled hair that bore subtle hints of gray at the temples, signifying wisdom and experience. The slight creases at the corners of his dark, slightly narrowed eyes told stories of many smiles and squints. His straight nose and the natural frown of his mouth gave him a serious demeanor as he handed her the stick.

"Here, just in case that breaks," he said with a knowing tone. He then turned to his son, "Dehai, let's work." With that, the servant said nothing else to her, and she observed them attentively watering and caring for the garden.

Dehai's hands were practiced, while his father's were worn and calloused, bearing the evidence of hard, earnest labor. Yinuo noted the defined wear in his face, the haggard appearance of a once-smooth complexion now etched with the marks of toil. His stubble was well-maintained. However, it could not hide the fatigue that clung to it. Though he resembled a villain from her children's fables with his serious demeanor, Yinuo understood from watching him that even those who appear scary can have genuine hearts. She shook her head, knowing better to judge people by their actions than their looks.

Initially, it was Dehai's eyes that had drawn her to him, but over time, his cleverness and heart deepened her affection. However, endless childhood appeared to the eyes of a girl in her milk years; her childhood was a transient song sung by nightingales and drooping peonies that came and went with the seasons. Dehai became a moment in her narrative, a thought hidden beneath her hair pin, behind her smile when peonies would bloom, and a name whispered in the soft words still clinging to her memories.

Present day

"Dehai," she whispered so softly, she did not know if she said the words. The man looked up. As fleeting as the peonies that once blossomed in the garden where they met. "Dehai is dead," the words echoed in her heart, a mantra of loss. The man sitting in the garden, caught her breath, stilled her world...This couldn't be him. This wasn't Dehai—she'd invaded a garden.

"Jiějiě! Yinuo! Where did you go!" her brother's voice cracked through her world, and she shot her head to it. She looked at the ghost of Dehai and then panicked, turning to find anything to escape. A gardening cart caught her eye, and she lunged towards it, running at full pace and pulling herself out of the garden just in time for her brother to miss her foot.

Ruijian panted out of breath. "E-excuse me, have you seen my sister?" he asked.

The man shook his head.

"Sorry to have bothered you!" Ruijian said, panicked, before rushing off back into the street.

A rustle of leaves brought the cool wind across man's face. Slowly, he stood up, struggling to maintain his balance.

He leaned on the chair before stabilizing his gait and getting on his toes to try and peer over the wall. Sadly, it was too tall.

"Heh," he chortled, amused by the woman. He brushed his ebony locks back over his shoulder as the door behind him opened, and an elder carrying a tray entered the garden.

"My lord, is everything all right?" the elder asked, looking over the wall.

"Which noble lords have daughters named Yinuo?"

"D-daughters?" he stuttered. The man smiled, patting his shoulder and carefully using it for support as he returned into his home and left the wheelchair in the lawn.

Engagements

2

Again, the arrows found their mark against the furthest targets from the platform with a *thunk—thunk—thunk*. Peering with an intense yet serene expression, Weixin stood with an imposing stature, a testament to his unmatched precision. Lord Yan's second son resembled him almost to a tee, carrying an angular jawline and defined cheekbones of the family's men. As their quickest servant ran to confirm his third consecutive bullseye, the back wall bore silent witness to his legacy; its surface poxed from the years from relentless practice.

Weixin exuded an air of calm confidence, his broad shoulders relaxing as he smoothly withdrew another arrow from the case.

Years of military service had not only influenced Weixin's attire but also his posture and composure. He wore his hair in a disciplined topknot and a practical black tunic with sleek sleeves adorned with a motif of a red tiger roaring down his left shoulder. As he awaited the signal to shoot again, his brother stood in contrast beside him.

Danbei's presence was notably more reserved, his oval face framed by a meticulously groomed hairstyle that fell loosely around his shoulders, embodying the ease of nobility rather than the rigidity of martial discipline. His piercing eyes reflected a quiet contemplation, mirroring the stillness of the spring air. The flight of cranes embroidered on his light-colored green tunic and pao lent him an air of grace and poise—more suited for court than exercise.

After a morning congested with ceremonial toasts and the weighty expectations of familial alliances, the relief that washed over Danbei was tangible as Weixin coaxed him to the familiar solitude of their training grounds. The sight of the old scoresheet held aloft by his younger brother offered a silent respite from the pressures of his impending nuptials. With a reserved smile, Danbei accepted the challenge, allowing the thrill of the match to momentarily dispel the heavy realities of his betrothal.

Weixin carefully adjusted his leather bracer, a piece as essential to his attire as his tunic, its surface etched with the scars of countless releases. Beside it, his thumb ring, intricately carved from jade, caught the light—embodying the concentrated essence of love and protection. This ring, gifted by his father on the day he joined the military, was more than a tool for archery but a profound token of affection. The light gleamed with his father's pride and imbued every draw of the bowstring with the weight of family honor and the protective love that bound them.

Four months had passed, during which Weixin's commitment to the military had kept him away. Now, as the brothers stood side by side, there was a sense of returning to a shared past. Dropping his pao into the arms of a waiting servant, Danbei reached for his long black bow to inspect the string as the servants rearranged the targets in an array of wiggled lines at varying heights. He selected a bamboo arrow from his quiver, examining the fletching—three feathers perfectly aligned for true flight. The arrowhead, pointed and made of forged iron, reflected his contemplative expression.

"Miss Lei, does seem lovely," Weixin commented to his brother, his well-shaped lips barely moving, as he retied a red ribbon onto his black bow. Danbei glanced over to the tie, catching Weixin's piercing gaze and the embroidery of his name on the red silks—Yinuo's handiwork, a parting gift from the last time Weixin had been home. The ribbon served Weixin as his stabilizer, a subtle reminder of whom he fought for. It'd saved his life once, binding a wound around his leg and preventing him from bleeding out.

"She is," Danbei dismissed, pulling to test the tautness of the bowstring, then lowering it to wait.

"But you're not satisfied," Weixin commented. *Thunk*— he landed another bullseye at the fresh target.

"Her family holds a high position in the court. I am merely worried *she won't* be satisfied," he replied.

Weixin drew in a deep breath, and slowly released it. "Your shot," he informed his brother, ignoring the comment about worthiness. Doubt wasn't something he liked to entertain as oftentimes doubt left men in his career dead. Though Weixin empathized with his brother's concerns, Lei Xing's ties to the general came with a promotion for him. He'd reached as far as he could in his career with the only hope of advancing was a familial tie.

General Lei made his name known for his renowned and skillful executions on and off the battlefield. Stories of the Mad Tiger inspired many young men to take up arms and join the service, especially with his exemplary records of preventing injuries and fewer lives lost. He was also aged, and his son hadn't joined the military. This was Weixin's chance to take the ties and advance his career.

For Danbei, the marriage seemed like a pragmatic and dutiful relation. He knew the courts and saw conflict coming. What better way to exhume control than to be behind the man who made the militant decisions? Besides, it wasn't just for the good of him and Weixin. All his brothers would benefit from the marriage to the general's daughter. If he could keep his new wife happy, but more so, it would promote his family and strengthen their ties. He shook his head and armed his bow, taking a side step over the line and shooting at his target. He'd missed the bullseye, but gained a respectable score. "Weixin, should I send Yinuo to learn more about her?" Danbei asked, preparing to take aim at the further target.

"No," Weixin replied curtly.

"And your reason?" Danbei asked, releasing the arrow and looking back towards Weixin, whose eyes darkened.

"General Lei's son is a leech," Weixin spat. Danbei was taken aback by this comment. The last he'd heard was that General Lei's son entered the Hall of Justice and was making a name for himself as a lawful man. "Your marriage opens up opportunities for wolves to seek out, mèimei. I do not wish for her to accidentally catch the eye of him. And if I am thigh deep in mud, reading about how you permitted Yinuo to marry him, I will hunt you down myself."

"Noted, dear brother," he replied, avoiding the confrontation.

Weixin exhaled his breath. "I know I will gain many sisters in our lifetime, but I am not ready to give away, Yinuo."

"You cannot keep her young forever," Danbei reminded him. "But I do understand where it's coming from. I will ensure to keep the leeches off her."

"And the wolves," he ordered.

"I will see what I can do, brother. Your shot," Danbei commented. As Weixin loosed his arrow, his attention was abruptly drawn to a flash of pink over the wall. "Yinuo!" he shouted, a surge of fear gripping him. There she was, perched precariously atop the wall, one leg dangling as she struggled to balance with the silk package.

"Mèimei!" Weixin called, rushing to her. "Arms down!" he shouted. The Second Young Master entered the archery range, bolting for his sister, who lost her balance and fell from the wall. Weixin caught her just in time. "Mèimei! Are you all right? Is your leg okay!" He asked frantically, steadying her.

"Yes, yes, thank you, Weixin, but I'm all right," she beamed to him, patting his shoulders. She was still caught in his arms.

"What are you doing coming from there! You know we practice archery here!"

"Eh, are you supposed to be practicing with the wedding so close?" she supplied her logic, and his brows furrowed. He shook his head and put an arm around her to march her to behind the archery line. He signaled all clear before sitting her down and picking up his bow.

"Do you have a death wish?" he asked. Yinuo shook her head, but knew better than to interrupt her brother. "What are you doing coming from behind that wall?"

Danbei had joined them in the conversation this time. He'd handed the bow to a servant. "Yes, I'd like to hear this as well."

She bit her lip, trying to find a reasonable explanation, but 'I was running from Ruijian' didn't have the same feel as 'I thought you weren't allowed to practice.' Her brothers honed in on her, both taking a side. While Weixin crossed his arms, Danbei kept his at his sides, both stances maintained a threatening presence that made Yinuo shrink. She'd swear they'd skin her alive if they didn't care so much about her. Yinuo held the wrapped silks closer to her body and flitted her eyes to Weixin, away from Danbei. Both were rather attuned to her secret language, and Weixin picked up on her anxiety before Danbei sighed.

"You went to fetch Lei Xing a present," Danbei stated. He relaxed a little, and a smile crept into the corner of his mouth. "Little Sister, you didn't have to do that."

"I did, though! Her father is a higher rank, and I wanted to make her feel welcome. I want her to like me. I didn't have an appropriate present for the granddaughter of a princess. And it's not just for Miss Lei—" Yinuo dropped her eyes to the hem of his robes. She'd been scared of not having as much time with Danbei, though it seemed now they barely had meals together with his position in the court.

Her brothers Danni, Ruijian, and Weixin's careers all took them away from the house. Danni had joined the priesthood. Ruijian spent most of his taking over his uncle's trade. Even Weixin's military career only granted him so many hours at home. Danbei's wedding brought her family back together for this brief moment, but she'd lose them all one by one again. So, she resolved that she had to make the most of it. Who knows when it would end?

"See, this is your fault," Weixin said to Danbei as he gently reassured his sister with a pat on her shoulder.

Danbei sighed, "Just because I'm the eldest..."

"Means I'm not in trouble for once," Weixin smiled broadly. "I'm sure your sister picked out a wonderful and appropriate gift. You should thank her." With that, Weixin focused his attention back to the targets, leaving Danbei to handle the conversation with Yinuo. He positioned his thumb, encased in the jade ring, around the bowstring and swiftly released the arrow, striking the target with precision.

Danbei sighed and brushed back his hair as Yinuo briefly glanced at his condition. While her brother maintained an air of reverence, today, she saw the darkness beneath his eyes and the tired look that aged him far more than he was. She even thought she saw gray hair, leaving her wondering how much stress he bared. Danbei returned her look with a strained smile and ordered a servant to bring him a chair. Now sitting beside her, he put out his hand for her; a childhood signal, she answered by threading her fingers to his, feeling his firm grip. "You missed her, by the way," he told her.

"I'm sorry, gēgē[9]," she said, shame hitting her. She looked away, defeated, as she felt her brother's reassuring grasp again.

"Don't be, even mother was taken by surprise by the visit. However much she would have appreciated having you with her, everything went well. Miss Lei and her family left quite pleased with the visit."

"Was mother upset?"

"En."

"Gēgē, will you—"

---

[9] "big brother"

"Oh, no. I'm not covering for this one. A man my age, especially one about to be married, shouldn't be out on the lawn."

"You do make a lovely lawn ornament, brother," Weixin teased as his arrow landed another bullseye. He shot a few more, aiming each at a different target and landing in the center every time. "Clear" was called, and the servants rushed to remove the arrows from the targets. He looked back at his sister. "Your turn, eldest brother," he said. Weixin switched seats with Danbei, allowing his brother to take up his bow. Weixin smiled, sitting down with his sister and calling for huángjiǔ wine from the servants.

"How many points did you get?" Danbei asked, eyeing the targets.

"All of them," Weixin smiled as he took the small cup and offered his sister one as well. "Do you want huángjiǔ[10], gēgē?"

"No, pour me another round of the General's báijiǔ[11]. You know I can't stand that sweet wine," Danbei said, focusing his shot again on the reset targets.

Yinuo smiled, "I'll try báijiǔ!"

Weixin flicked her on the nose. "You know better, mèimei."

---

[10] Sweet fermented wine made from grains.
[11] Traditional Chinese strong alcoholic drink.

Yinuo rubbed her nose and returned his warm smile. "Weixin ge, who else knows I went out?"

"Did you go out?" He feigned, tapping his lip and winking at her. "We found you here pouting and decided to keep you company."

"Thank you, Weixin."

"No worries, mèimei," he reassured her with a brilliant smile. The warmth of the huángjiǔ flushed her cheeks as she sipped it slowly, savoring the rich, slightly fruity taste. Her brother, Weixin, alternated between huángjiǔ and báijiǔ, though his marksmanship never faltered. He led the challenge by a few scores until he got bored and let Danbei win the last few rounds.

As the servants cleared the field and organized the equipment, the sun began to set. Yinuo stretched, resting her head on the back of her hand, and looked to her brothers, who continued conversing in a low drone. "I think we got her drunk, little brother," Danbei remarked.

"It would appear so," he replied.

Yinuo groaned, "I'm not drunk. I'm just warm."

"Ah, yes, dear sister," Danbei teased. "Weixin, go fetch Yaolin. We should get Yinuo to bed."

Yinuo waved her hand. "No, I'm fine. I'm still awake. Your conversation just got boring."

"En. That definitely means it's time to rest, mèimei," Weixin remarked. He rose from his seat and headed towards the servants, leaving Yinuo and Danbei together. Danbei sipped his wine calmly, his eyes nearly closed. Yinuo observed him, caught in the warm glow of the setting sun behind him, the sweet fragrance of magnolias in the air.

"Gēgē," she whispered. "He leaves..."

"I know, Little Yi," Danbei replied.

"He's coming back, right?" she asked, tears ebbing at the corners of her eyes. She brushed her cheek and shook her head. "Danbei..."

"Yes, Little Yi?" he responded softly, his eyes closed, his hand poised on the delicate cup between his thumb and forefinger.

"I saw Dehai again," she whispered. At this, her brother's posture stiffened; he straightened in his chair, his brows knitting together as he focused on Yinuo, who looked away longingly. He did not see the woman before him, with her cheeks rounded and flushed from the warmth of huángjiǔ, nor the spirited glint that resided in her warm, almond-shaped eyes. Her inky hair cascaded in soft waves over her shoulders, framing a face that had gracefully absorbed the essence of her beauty. The dim lighting highlighted the elegant contours of her femininity and gleamed off the softness of her slightly curved lips—lips that were always smiling, even when downtrodden. No, Danbei did not see the woman before him; instead, he saw an image of his little sister—with her leg bandaged, her rugose hanfu, and tear trails marring her face. He shook the image from his head and reached for her hand, but she recoiled.

"I know he's dead," she whispered. "It must have been a coincidence..."

"Who are you talking about?" Danbei asked, his voice tight with concern.

"In the peony garden...the one I fell into. He was there," she said, smiling faintly. "No, he wasn't there; it was someone else with a deep scar on his brow and a smaller one on his chin. It couldn't have been Dehai, right, brother?"

"En," Danbei replied, squeezing her hand. "Let's get you inside; you can dream and forget about him."

"Yes, I will forget about Dehai..." Yinuo confirmed, but her heart rebuked it with a lurch. Weixin returned with the maid, Yaolin, who helped steady the young miss and escorted her away from her brothers. Weixin took Yinuo's seat as Danbei watched her struggle to walk.

"What is it?" Weixin inquired, "Brother, what's with that face?"

"Nothing, just a coincidence. Another round?" Danbei offered in attempt to divert the conversation. Weixin took the wine bottle from him and poured the clear liquid carefully into his clouded cup.

Shooting Pain

3

The rain always sent shooting pain through her leg. It'd been like this since childhood when she first woke up screaming in a thunderstorm. As an adult, though, Yinuo simply groaned awake, carefully pushing herself from her bed and tracing her thigh with her fingertips—the pressure nearly enough to ease the pain as she grimaced. She couldn't remember how she'd gotten to her room, the early morning darkness causing her vision to struggle to adjust.

Slowly, she tried to stand, reaching for the crutch at the side of her bed. It had been weeks since she last required its support, but today, the sharp flare reminded her of her dependency. Yinuo chided herself, suspecting it was the two falls the day prior that had aggravated her condition. The crutch bore her brother Ruijian's trademark. Crafted only from the finest sandalwood, a material favored for its durability and exquisite grain. He's spent hours smoothing it to perfection and applying the layers of lustrous lacquer that Yinuo could feel even in her tender grasp. The top was cushioned with down and wrapped in red silk, a luxurious touch ensuring comfort with every use. It was one of the first gifts he had crafted for her, a symbol of care she turned to whenever the rains came or the pain resurfaced.

She never believed she would live with pain when she was a child, but there it was as she stumbled in the dark for her medicine on the desk across her room. Carefully, she aimed for the desk when a sharp throb seized her leg, and she fell with a clash against the floor. A pounding of feet came rushing towards her.

"Jiějiě!" Mingdan called. "Are you all right?" Yinuo curled up, rubbing her upper thigh and cursing the intense ache spreading through her leg. She squinted her eyes shut and took some calming breaths before Mingdan's hand offered her the medicine she desired.

"What are you doing up so early?" she asked him.

"I have yet to retire for the evening," he confessed. Mingdan's room was the closest to hers, and he'd responded when she'd fallen before.

"Thank you," she replied, accepting the willow bark. He then gently assisted her, taking her arm to help her into a nearby chair. The room filled with the sound of steady rain, punctuated by the occasional crack of lightning. Mingdan moved to the candles, lighting them before turning back to face her, his lips pursed and brow furrowed with concern.

"Should I summon the physician?" he asked.

"No, it's the same old pain, Mingdan. It'll clear up when the storm's passed."

He put the back of his thumb to his lips, not satisfied with her answer but unsure on how to proceed. "Should I alert mother?"

Again, she shook her head. "I'll be okay. Mingdan, go get some rest."

"Yinuo..." he started, but stopped. "Fine, I'll abide by your wishes." Mingdan wore a white tunic cinched at the waist by a simple belt decorated with golden thread in an ornate interlocking pattern. The billowing sleeves tapered gracefully to his wrists. Simplistic yet refined. Mingdan kept his hair neat, swept up and away from his angular jaw, and held in place by a silver hairpiece that gleamed in the warm candle's hue. Yinuo's gaze lingered on his hands, covered in streaks of black ink matching the wear beneath his reflective, rich brown eyes. Mingdan always did have such kind, looking glass eyes.

Without a word, he stepped out, only to return promptly, balancing a tome, an inkwell, a brush, and a scroll. With these in hand, he made himself comfortable at her desk and started reviewing the classic text.

"I'm okay, Mingdan," she said to him.

"En," he replied, "I merely remain nearby, should you require my presence. Besides, this riddle is perplexing me, and I think better with company."

"Oh, so that's why you're up. You never were someone who could stop until you've found a solution," she said. He continued to focus on the tome, not answering her. Yinuo carefully tested the weight of her leg on the floor and, taking up Ruijian's crutch, stood slowly and limped back to bed. She threw the covers over herself, watching Mingdan illuminated by the warm candlelight at the desk. He would never admit it, but Yinuo knew he worried the most for her, really, enough for everyone. Any task he faced was done so with meticulous research and preparation.

However, he was also the quietest of her brothers, expressing himself more through the written word than speech. His brilliant mind had been apparent since childhood, and the family had supported his pursuit of knowledge in every way—except for allowing him to leave for formal tutelage. Yinuo saw this in the subtle fidget of his leg, his yearning for the mountains described in his books, the histories, and the places beyond their reach. She knew if he ever left to seek a wise shifu who could expand his horizons beyond the court, he might never return, ensnared by the allure of a distant city or the majesty of an ancient riverfront. And so, Mingdan remained, his intellect bound within the pages of his texts, living vicariously through the stories of others instead of roaming the vast world he longed to see.

Yinuo called to him. "When do you take your exams?"

"Soon, jiějiě," he replied, turning a page, but never breaking contact for her.

"Do you think you'll get a good score?"

"It is my intent," he replied.

"When you pass, accept a position someplace far away, Mingdan, and write to me everyday of the wonders you see along the way. That would make me happy."

He smiled, "My position will be here, close to father and eldest brother."

"No, you could go anywhere you wanted with your score. Why stay here, brother?"

"You're here," he supplied.

Yinuo rolled her eyes, "And what if, when I'm married, I am sent someplace far away? Wouldn't there be no excuse for you to stay?"

His eyes never left the page as he spoke. "You're raising this topic as a diversion from your discomfort. The medicine should take effect shortly. By the way, Danbei mentioned you've brought him a gift."

"Do not change the subject, little brother! Think on it, please."

He relented with a sigh. "Only for you, Yinuo. However, did you really leave yesterday to fetch a gift?

"Yes, for Miss Lei," Yinuo said, then panicked. "The gift! Mingdan, you must help me find it!"

"Where did you have it last?" he asked.

"At the archery range! Oh no, we have to find it! It's precious, and if I lose the gift, it'll all be for naught!" Yinuo tried to stand but started to fall when Mingdan jutted from his desk, just in time to prevent it. He didn't ask if she was all right or rebuke her desire to find the gift. He simply saw the determination in his sister's eyes.

"En," he replied, sliding her crutch beneath her arm. He lifted her shoes from their stand and helped her put them on. Then, he held the door aloft as she passed through.

Together, Mingdan and Yinuo walked towards the archery field, Mingdan carrying a lantern he had left outside her room. This early in the morning, the vast estate of the Yans was deserted, a complex of multiple buildings and various rooms, all enclosed by a masoned wall, resembling a small fortress. The considerable size a daunting thought, Mingdan entertained as he accompanied his ailing sister hastening to the training grounds. They darted from cover to cover, seeking protection from the rain, until they noticed a warm light emanating from an outer building—a place both Mingdan and Yinuo knew was supposed to be empty.

Mingdan covered his lantern, dimming the light, and pulled his sister to his side. They saw two shadows within the window conversing in low tones.

"Are you sure she said *Dehai*?" A man spoke through the storm. Yinuo didn't recognize the voice, and before she could ask Mingdan, he had her pressed up against the side of the window with her mouth covered. Mingdan listened intently, carefully maneuvering them to avoid being spotted, all the while assessing the intentions of the men whose forms were only partially visible, obscured by a screen that cast their shadows.

The response of the other, was too low to hear, and interrupted by a slam of hands against a table. "Do not tell anyone what you know!" the man hissed.

Again, silence, but the only person she had told was Danbei. Who would be interested in a mere servant? She tried to peer into the room, but Mingdan's grip held her stationed in place.

"We will look into this. It is too soon to make rash decisions," the man said.

Mingdan swore under his breath as the door creaked open unexpectedly, swiftly pulling his sister into the shadows to conceal them. His hand remained firmly over her mouth, silencing any gasps of fear, while his eyes tracked the ominous figure meticulously. It wasn't just the suddenness of the stranger's movement that chilled Yinuo to the bone—it was the figure itself. A man, if one could call him that, draped in a black cape that fluttered like the wings of a night creature, his face obscured by a large-brimmed hat that cast his features into eerie darkness. As he prowled the outer wall with an unsettling grace, his presence seemed to slice through the stormy air. For a moment, his silhouette paused, as if sensing their watchful eyes, before he vanished into the night.

"Why would they care about, Dehai?" she asked stunned, faltering as the last of her strength left her legs, and quickly her brother responded by gently lowering her to her knees.

"Stay here," Mingdan ordered his sister, but she clutched his hands, her eyes filled with pleading.

"No, Mingdan, don't go."

"You'll only hinder me with your bad leg. Remain here; I shall return shortly."

"What are you going to do! Please, Mingdan!"

He gave her a smile and a pit formed at the bottom of her stomach. Without a word, he slipped from her grasp, leaving her to the cold and pain around her.

A boom of thunder brought her back to her childhood, when the rain smacked her face as the horse beneath her bucked and reared against her tiny taps. "Go horse!" She shouted into the tempest, her voice barely rising above the howling wind. "Go, we must save him! Go!" She pleaded again and again for the horse to move, but it labored through the rain, trudging at its own pace. Fear gripped her so tightly she wasn't sure she could endure the pain constricting her chest. She cried out, begging, "Please, horse!"

A crack of lightning spooked the beast, and in the next moment, Yinuo found herself sprawled in the mud, the horse rearing above her. She rolled away just in time to dodge its smashing hooves and picked herself up, watching as it galloped off into the night. Yinuo struggled to her feet, each step a battle, as her injured leg protested every movement, her determination the only fuel driving her forward into a blind run.

Reaching the execution grounds, she was panting, dragging her leg, as the cold mingled with the sweat on her brow. Her small form dwarfed by the imposing white stone walls and gravel path, towering so high, she could see only the storm clouds churning above. She ran blindly down the corridors until she reached an iron gate, which, to her dismay, was not open as expected. Desperation lending her strength, she threw her shoulder against the door, pounding with all her might until the guards, taking pity on her, finally pushed it open for her to pass.

There, at the base of the massive stairs, she saw the platform, with blood and hay scattered everywhere. The crowd's presence and the sickening beat of drums reverberated off the walls. Little Yinuo elbowed her way through, her small frame jostled by indifferent bodies. "Dehai!" she screamed, unable to see the platform due to her stature. Surrounded by a blur of pao and angry faces, she struggled through—a tiny voice in a crowd of silks and rain, unheard.

Then, a loud crash,

the crowd's cheers,

and a *speck of red* on her cheek

became her entire world.

"Dehai is dead."

As lightning cleaved the sky once more, its fleeting brilliance forced Yinuo to confront the relentless downpour, prompting her to brush away the solitary droplet from her cheek. Kneeling there, drenched and numb, she lost track of time as the memory of the execution seared itself into her consciousness. "Dehai is dead. Dehai is dead. Dehai is dead." The words echoed like a haunting refrain, grounding her in the sorrow that remained.

She'd lost her best friend. She'd failed to save him. And no matter how much her family attempted to absolve her of blame, insisting it wasn't her fault, that a child could not take responsibility for what had happened—she did. If she did not acknowledge, "Dehai is dead," she would tempt herself into believing in a falsehood, a hope that would only leave her tortured as the truth progressed. But it did not stop her from wishing and praying to anyone who would listen that she'd be with her king of flowers again.

Omens

④

Grandmother Pei visited last night. She often came when Yinuo's life changed, during special occasions such as her first cycle, when she gripped her stomach so tightly she thought she'd die, or on Double Seventh when she expressed her pride for her. This night, she wiped the speck from her cheek and called her "precious" and "her little one," over and over again until she felt her lips on her forehead and the embrace of her cool arms.

"My precious one," Nainai whispered, kissing the top of her head. Her grandmother had left the world peacefully in a dream before her eighth winter, and though still hard, her loss did not compare to the pain of losing Dehai. He'd been severed from her—an altogether different pain to cope with than when Nainai fell into a dreamless sleep, and Dehai was forced into death. So when she reflected on it, Nainai's passing only brought a brief melancholy thought that vanished in the next.

Yinuo groaned, feeling the cool cloth on her head. Alongside her, Danni read the Zhuangzi with a thoughtful hand on his cheek. She moaned and slowly sat up in bed, catching Danni's attention from his text, his presence a calming force in the sun shafts of early afternoon. The storm had passed, and with it, the pain in her leg.

He wore a zhiju made of natural hemp in a hue of deep indigo. The fabric, modest and coarse to the touch, draped softly around him—a far cry from the attire Danni wore in his wild years. A faint smile graced his lips, and his eyes, gently curved like the delicate arch of a willow leaf and reflective as a tranquil pond, met hers with warmth.

"Did you enjoy your nap?" Danni inquired with a softspoken tone, and eyes focused on his tome.

"Nap?" she asked, still wiping the sleep from her eyes. Her clothes were dry and warm, and the room heated slightly to her comfort. Danni sat near her table and marked his page with a red ribbon.

"Father and the other brothers have been called to work," he informed her.

"Even Weixin? I thought he had time off?" she asked.

Danni nodded, "He is answering General Lei's summons and won't be back until evening. This is a good thing, sister. How are you feeling?"

"I'm... where's Mingdan? What happened to my gift, that stranger! Danni! Where is Mingdan!"

"He's fine. Mingdan went with Sile to his lessons early this morning. Oh, yes, that's right." He rose from the chair and picked up the silk bundle at her bedside. "Mingdan found this for you and says that the visitor last night was a friend of the family."

"Friend?" she canted her head and then shook it. Last night, the visitor seemed so threatening, and there was something off about the gleam of his eyes. "They brought up Dehai," she said.

"Yes, I'm sorry, dear sister. Just forget about it. You overindulged last night and weren't feeling well when you awoke. I'm certain that you were just influenced by the huángjiǔ Weixin kept pouring." He sighed and shook his head in an annoyed way. "Our brothers should know better to avoid the second bottle."

"I take it Yaolin's been here," she said, wrapping the quilt around her shoulders.

"En. She has an errand to run in town for mother. If you want to join her today, I will leave you to get dressed. She's leaving soon."

"Oh..." Yinuo still didn't know if her mother's temper had simmered or merely sizzled out. "Thank you, Danni."

Danni bowed to her, picked up his copy of the Zhuangzi, and headed for the door, sliding it closed and allowing Yinuo a moment to breathe. She didn't usually dress herself, but with Yaolin busy, she hurried to make herself ready and then grabbed her pink shoes with the peach blossoms on the edge. Expectantly, her leg wasn't hurting today, so she rushed through the hallway quickly but did not run as she passed her mother's study.

Peering in cautiously, like a cat to a stranger, Yinuo watched from a distance as her mother slid her porcelain hand over her ebony hair and tucked the loose strand behind her ear. She would always be her mother, even if the crow's feet faintly started to form at the side of her round eyes and the wrinkles touched her smile lines. Slightly overweight, but expected for a woman who'd bared seven children and lost one.

Her mother's chestnut-colored eyes caught hers in the golden mirror and then quickly diverted to her desk. "Are you better?" she asked shortly.

"Yes, mother," she replied.

Her mother capped the perfume bottle and then carefully stood and turned to her, folding her arms. "Little Yi'er, what am I going to do with you?"

"Love me?" she offered, and her mother chuckled.

Her mother did not look amused as she struck her with the back of her hand to her shoulder. It didn't hurt, but was enough of a warning for her to quiet. "I do love you, Yinuo. You spent the night drinking with your elder brothers."

"Weixin's hand was a little heavy."

"A little?" the vein in her mother's forehead twitched. "You ran out into the rain this morning, and you better thank your brother Mingdan when he returns this afternoon. If he hadn't been up, he wouldn't have seen you sleepwalking!"

So, that's the excuse her brother used, Yinuo thought, silently adding to her scroll another time her brothers had covered for her. One of these days, she would unravel it, and it would reach from the Great Hall all the way out of town. With downcast eyes, Yinuo carefully took her mother's hand and rubbed the space between her forefinger and thumb.

"It was important to spend time with them," Yinuo explained.

"Honestly, I should be lecturing your brothers instead," her mother said, but Yinuo quickly shook her head.

"Mother, please don't be vexed. I'm feeling fine and would love to go with you to the market. I'll help with the wedding preparations in any way I can."

For a while, her mother weighed Yinuo's words but didn't initially agree or disagree. However, today didn't seem to favor Yinuo. "And reward you for sneaking out? Don't give me that look; I coaxed it from Danbei and Weixin. Yinuo, you're not leaving until your groom picks you up," she huffed, then called for her maid and started out the door.

"Mother!" she chased after her. "It was—"

"I won't hear it. Yinuo, spend time with Danni today. At least he won't let you stray from the path of virtue." Her mother left the estate, loading herself into a covered carriage with red lacquer and intricate carvings. Yaolin appeared, nodding at the lady of the house before putting up an arm in front of Yinuo, their shared look serving as a signal to watch over her. Something didn't feel right about the exchange, even though her mother had asked Yaolin since her childhood to watch over her. There was tension in the crease of her brow and a stiffening to her body. Whatever it was, her mother was hiding something from her.

Yinuo shook her head and marched off. Fine, she'd spend time with Danni. She found him at the family shrine, softly murmuring a prayer as he meditated, kneeling. Quietly approaching, she intended to kneel beside him but misstepped, her hand instinctively reaching for his shoulder to steady herself. Her touch didn't disrupt his meditation; instead, Danni's hand found hers, steadying her until she managed to kneel beside him. He gave her hand a reassuring squeeze before gently letting go.

After concluding his prayer, Danni inhaled deeply, marking the end. "She's still upset."

"She's acting weird, gēgē," Yinuo replied. "I haven't seen her act this way since she lost the baby and was keeping it from us."

"She has her reasons," Danni supplied. "She's our mother; when the time is right, she will share with us if she believes it will promote our wellbeing."

"I hate seeing her like that," Yinuo said.

He nodded, "When we are young, we're oblivious to most concerns, and then one day we notice it, but instead of coming in on a joke, we realize the discomfort and empathize with the hurt. How is your leg feeling, by the way?" he asked.

"It's fine," she said.

"Good," he smiled to her. "Mèimei, what's wrong?"

"Wrong?" she tilted her head.

"Don't be like Mother; tell me what troubles you."

Yinuo looked to the family shrine, and thought about it. For one, there was the memory of Dehai, and two, the strangeness of her brothers and mother. She felt like her life was shrouded, and it made her fearful of something ominous approaching. It didn't help her dreams.

Danni had never been this compassionate in youth. He fought wildly with Ruijian and oftentimes would whine about the smallest of things. Among his friends, Danni was the one who caused trouble and thought it fun to dare others into dangerous situations. He never intentionally hurt someone, and his words were more callous than calm back then. There was a lot of injustice he couldn't change, but always he'd seen himself as her elder brother and caretaker.

"Danni, do you remember, Dehai?" she asked.

"No," he hesitated before lying to her. "Why do you ask?"

"I think he's haunting me," she sighed as if saying the words released the tension in her chest. She breathed through the rest of the thought. "An omen, perhaps, to some life change if I keep seeing him? Or perhaps it is just the season of peonies and I'm too sentimental," she confided in her brother. Who held onto his prayer beads and whispered a prayer to the incense he burned at the family shrine. Yinuo savored the sweetness of rŭxiāng[12] filling the chamber as Danni prayed.

"It could be," he said. "You should listen. We all would benefit from listening," She hadn't remembered when he'd been so insightful as a child. Danni, as a child, was always in

---

[12] Aroma of frankincense, used in incense.

trouble, brash, rash, and wild. She could scarcely believe the calm and dignified priest who now kneeled before her family's shrine with such a serious expression. Danni stood and offered her a hand, helping her to rise with him, his smile warm against the backlight from the door.

"Come here," he said, guiding her to a side table and selecting a piece of paper from the stack. He scribed a talisman, murmured a prayer, and then handed it to her. "There, no more evil spirits will come near you today."

"Thanks, Danni," she said, tucking it carefully away. They walked together out to the garden, where the rich scent of peonies thickly penetrated the air. Yinuo turned to the sky, taking a deep breath, as her brother paced a few steps ahead; the moment of solace was a balm for the pain that had gripped her that morning. Her crutch, now redundant, lay forgotten in her room.

Danni's pace stemmed, each step purposely taken in mindfulness of Yinuo. He paused occasionally to admire the peach blossoms and, from time to time, take a fragrant cutting or two, handing her the branches to carry.

"Danni," she called to him.

"Yes, mèimei," he noted thoughtfully as he prepared the branches with a smile.

"Eldest brother's marriage will open discussions for my own, correct?"

"It's possible," he replied.

"Will you find me a husband far away? Perhaps, near your temple where I can at least be close to you."

"It's a long distance," he replied.

"I know, but I keep dreaming of leaving for a distant home, almost to the point where I drift out into the sea and never return. So if this is an omen, I'd rather be near my family, even if far away."

"Father will not allow it," he reassured her. "You are not going to be sent so far."

"Then why do I dream of the vast sea?"

"I do not know. Perhaps it is because of something else entirely. What else have you dreamt of recently?"

"A forest," she replied, "So dark and grand, the leaves envelop me in shadows as if night itself has descended. I'm overwhelmed by the darkness, and I find myself calling out for my family like a lost child. I don't know what it means, gēgē," she confided in him. Turning to the peonies in the garden, she found one with a particularly large head. Its rich fuchsia color called to her, and the deep fragrance of the petals enveloped her senses. "I'm nervous," she admitted.

"Don't be," he replied. "Wherever you go, Little Yi, you will be strong. I know it. You're the only girl I know who, after breaking her leg riding a horse, would then beg her brothers to teach her to ride again."

"I'm weird."

"No," he retorted. "Your Yinuo, brave and perhaps reckless, but never weird."

"What do you think it all means?" she asked.

"Are you asking as my sister or seeking a philosophical answer?" he replied, temporarily taking the peach branches from her to bundle them with a red ribbon before handing them over. He then stepped back. "Well?"

"I respect your council, and you know I would never ask *little* Danni for advice."

"I have grown a few chi," he chuckled. "But as to your question. I think you're dealing with grief, sister. The wedding of our brother is a change in our lives, but it will bring happiness as well as trials. You are right to be nervous, because if you were not then it would show that you did not care. Besides, I saw Danbei's new carved mandarin ducks. You only have the best wishes for your eldest brother."

"And my dreams?" she prodded.

"Do not burden yourself with needless worry; it will all be clear when it arrives. Whatever, we face, you have us at your side. Now, let's go find lunch. I'm starving and I know you haven't eaten yet."

"That sounds lovely, gēgē," she replied, as her stomach gave a protest. She blushed, and Danni laughed, leading them towards the kitchens. Yinuo followed behind, holding onto her peach blossom bundle and stopping only a moment to look behind her. She could have sworn she'd seen something in her peripheral vision, but it vanished with her brother's call, beckoning her back into the house.

With her brother's wedding approaching, the tasks around the house appeared more and more laborious. Yinuo assisted her mother in sewing tablecloths, gathering and arranging flowers for the centerpieces, and shadowing her as she directed the servants in preparing special menu items. Additionally, her mother ensured that the preferences of the invited families were taken into account to maintain harmony. She found herself after the evening meal, completely exhausted, lounging on a chair with a bowl of star fruit slices she'd carefully cut up and snuck from the kitchens to munch on.

For three days, the "something" watched her. At first, she thought it was a magpie outside or even a shadow in the corner, but as more days passed, she became more certain that the entity saw her. Moreover, whatever it was, the "something" knew that she was aware of it. Yet, when she brought it up to Yaolin, she was reprimanded for making up stories about flickering light.

Instead, her father ordered more guards to protect the manor, taking it upon himself to ensure everything had been prepared correctly for the ceremony. There were rites and traditions that Danni helped prepare, as well as entertaining the family arriving days too early. It left the estate bustling with excitement and the color red everywhere.

Yinuo heard the maids approaching with happy chatter and decided to leap behind the side of the lounger. She'd just finished dusting and organizing Mingdan's library for Cousin Bing's futon and wasn't ready to be swept up into yet another task. Carefully, she jutted out her hand to grab the tip of her porcelain bowl and made her way out of the room.

On her hands and knees, she crept out the door and towards the peony garden. Slipping between the thick jade stalks that lined the back wall, she pressed her head against it. For a moment, relief washed over her as she savored the crisp, tangy slices, their juice cooling her throat.

"Little Yi!" she heard Yaolin and froze mid-bite of the translucent, star-shaped piece. "Your father is looking for you! Oh, where did she go? Little Yi!"

Yinuo dropped to the gravel, certain she heard a chuckle just as her elbow resonated against the stones. Too focused on locating the source, she barely registered the stinging pain or noticed anything beyond the plants. A slow, uncomfortable feeling traced through her gut. Promptly, she sprang from the peonies, crashing right into the back of Maid Yaolin.

"Umph! Yi'er! What are you doing there?" Yaolin said, flustered.

"I...dropped my star fruit."

"Dropped your star fruit?" the watchful eyes of Yinuo weren't ready to believe her, but it was true; her bowl now resided in the back of the peonies to be feasted on by crickets.

Yinuo sighed, "I may have been avoiding work. Honestly, why doesn't father ask his capable sons?"

"Do not question your father, and everyone in this family is busy with Danbei's wedding. But that is neither here nor now. Your father has summoned you."

"Summoned me? Sounds serious. What did I do wrong?" Yinuo asked. Had her escapade outside the walls finally come to light? Well, she couldn't hide the silks and carved mandarin ducks forever. She'd given them to her mother, who not only complimented her on the purchase but ensured her that the baby clothes made from them would be "quite" suitable for a great-grandson of a princess. Yinuo felt pride at that moment, but it was currently being overshadowed by a rather forceful Yaolin who grabbed her arm and marched her towards the main hall.

Yaolin paused, licked her fingers, and tidied Yinuo's eyebrows, then proceeded to brush the dust off her shoulders and straighten her pleated skirt. "Stop, it's fine," Yinuo protested.

"Shh!" Yaolin hushed, firmly guiding Yinuo back to face the door and skillfully adjusting her peony pin in her hair. After giving Yinuo a thorough final inspection, Yaolin's demeanor softened.

"Master Yan, your daughter, Yan Yinuo, is here in response to your summons," Yaolin announced with a soft eloquence that made Yinuo curious about who was so important on the other side of the screen door.

"Enter!" a voice boomed from beyond the door. It was a tone she hadn't heard in a long time, its authority making the hairs on the back of her neck stand straight, just like her posture. She folded her arms as Yaolin gave Yinuo one last warning glance before the doors slid open on their own.

Yinuo entered the Great Hall, the heart of their home and the most prestigious space in the entire house. This hall, representing the Yan family to the outside world, served not just as a venue for hosting guests but also as a showcase of their pride. Typically maintained with care, its decoration for the wedding now rivaled the opulence of a prince's estate, filled with the fresh scent of orange and peach blossom branches—remnants of Yinuo and Danni's recent visit.

At the hall's end, her parents were seated side by side in elevated rosewood chairs with a tea set on a small table between them. Kneeling on a pillow before them, Yinuo observed two men: one, an elderly figure whose stature was lost in the folds of blue refined silk; the other, clad in a light yellow pao, splendidly embroidered with large peonies.

Standing behind them, she saw the elaborate hairpiece the younger man wore and noticed the peony motif repeated in the golden design. For a moment, she thought, she saw him twitch to face her, but the man knelt firm, his hands in his lap. Yinuo heard the doors closing behind her and the soft taps of her slippers on the polished marble tiles. She felt the whole world slow down as if approaching a moment from which she thought it better to flee. Out the window, before the stage, Yinuo witnessed a nightingale perched among the peach blossoms fly out of frame.

"Yinuo," her mother breathed, and it brought her back to the moment. She took a few steps forward and avoided making direct eye contact with the men. Off to the side where she usually sat hung a privacy screen of linen lace that she knew she should have approached but didn't. Instead, she knelt and bowed to her father in line with the men.

"You've called for me?" she asked.

"Take your seat," her father said evenly. Yinuo stood, her tapping feet the only sound in the entire room. She sat down in her chair and observed the scene before her, now blurred by the screen. At least the voices were clear.

"Yinuo, this is Lord Nie and his son Prince Cuilin," her father's voice was tight and stressed.

"A pleasure," she responded, giving a slight bob of her head.

"They have come to make a proposition, and I would hear an explanation, Yinuo," her father started but suddenly stopped as her mother's hand caught his arm.

"Do not be so quick to anger," her mother warned, eying the two men in front of her. "It is unconventional, but it is not outright wrong."

"I understand your reservations, Lord Yan," Lord Nie's soft voice entered the scene, almost like a cat purring. "We come before you not merely as suitors among many but as the most fitting and advantageous match for Miss Yan."

Suitors? Yinuo's heart skipped a beat. Did he just say suitors! She felt sick and placed her hand at her mouth to suppress a gasp.

"Yet, consider the fortuitous nature of this connection. Our families share a bond of mutual respect and aligned interests, and you know my Cuilin is not only my son but also a Prince of Zhou. The union between Prince Cuilin and Yinuo could only strengthen our ties, presenting a formidable alliance. In these uncertain times, such a bond could prove invaluable, ensuring prosperity and security for both our houses."

"You mean to marry her to the hostage prince," Lord Yan interjected.

"Hostage is such a cruel word for such a distinguished son," Lord Nie countered. Yinuo cursed the screen before her, wishing only to see the prince's reaction to this exchange more clearly.

"And what of you, prince! What can you offer my daughter besides a casket of sorrow?"

"Husband!"

"You come to us before my eldest's marriage is sealed and demand the hand of my only daughter as if you're scavengers early to a feast. I am sure there are other suitors more palatable than that of Prince Cuilin."

"We do not mean to offend," came Cuilin's low voice, breaking the sanctity of the room. She heard her father gasp, and for a moment, she wanted to hear Prince Cuilin's voice again.

"My Prince, remember the customs here differ," Lord Nie softly purred.

"What is different? A prince sees a flower he desires and seeks her father's permission solely because it is the right thing to do. Your daughter has invaded my garden, and since then, I have not had a moment's rest. You call me 'hostage,' yet you also address me as 'prince'; therefore, I command your respect," his voice shot her father down. Almost low and grueling, it captivated Yinuo. Instead of fearing his possessiveness, she found herself admiring his boldness.

"Have I invaded your garden?" she spoke up.

The men did not turn to her but lowered their heads in a bow. "Young miss," Cuilin softly replied. "These talks are too preemptive for your presence. I am sorry for the distress, please, do not mind me."

"Tell me, prince. Why me?"

He paused, and a long silence followed as if he were crafting a story or searching for the words. His visage was damnably shrouded by the gauze before her, but she was focusing on his low voice and the gentleness that had previously been directed toward her.

"That is enough. Yinuo, the prince, makes a valid point. Lord Nie, this is not the time to invest my daughter. You are welcome to stay for the wedding, but I will not entertain any propositions until my son is married into General Lei's family."

"As you wish, thank you for hearing us," he bowed deeply. "Prince Cuilin, let us retire."

"En, this discussion has yet to reach its conclusion."

"I will not see you out," her father answered. The two lifted from the floor and headed towards the main doors.

From her angle, Yinuo caught a glimpse of his profile. "Dehai," she whispered. It was the same man she had seen in the garden. Lord Nie's frail body leaned against Prince Cuilin's, but their movement betrayed them. It wasn't the old man who needed support but Prince Cuilin himself. Recalling the spokes of Cuilin's wheelchair, Yinuo confirmed that the prince needed support in walking, even if others in the room were fooled by the facade. Her focus only heightened, recognizing that the prince was moments from collapsing, which only grew her admiration for the steps he continued to take. She turned to her father just as she heard the door slide closed.

"I'll fetch the good china," she said.

"You'll do no such thing," her father cut in. "Yinuo!"

Yinuo stood before her father could lecture her, heading for a side door instead of the one the prince had left from. Sneaking her way through the house, she exited close to the front doors, where she looked for the prince and Lord Nie. Stopping at the corner of the house, she peered into the front courtyard, seeing her brother Danbei welcome Prince Cuilin.

"I am glad you made it, Prince Cuilin," Danbei said with a revered and gentle smile. Yinuo pressed herself further into the wall, watching from a distance.

"Congratulations on your engagement to General Lei's daughter," Cuilin replied smoothly, the low tone still enthralling her.

"Yes, truly a joyous occasion. We look forward to the ceremony," Lord Nie explained as he faltered on his left leg in pretense. "Ah, excuse these frail bones. We must retire for the evening, I'm afraid."

"Of course, a room has been prepared, and we look forward to hosting you. Please let us know if there is anything we can do to make the Zhou Prince comfortable."

"You are indeed gracious," he replied.

"Who are you watching?" Sile's voice touched her ear. She slapped him and pressed her fingers to her lips. In response, her youngest brother flailed, looking almost indignant as he dropped his school tome. Yinuo blocked him from seeing what she saw.

"Jiějiě? Who is that?" he peered from behind the wall and over her head. Unfortunately, Sile towered above her, leaving her little option but to lung at him and pull him down to her size. Her focus turned to watching as Prince Cuilin pretended to struggle with Lord Nie.

"He hurts," Yinuo said softly, easing her grip on her brother.

"Again, who is that?" he whispered.

"I don't know," she shook her head, "He tried to proposition marriage to father for me."

"WHAT!"

"Sh!" Yinuo panicked and covered his mouth as a slew of words flew from her brother into her hand. She pulled him into a side room, losing track of Prince Cuilin.

"Let go of my mouth!" Sile broke free and readjusted himself. "Stop being so crazy! Ugh, what is on your hands? Did you eat star fruit?"

"That's not the point! I..." Yinuo blushed a crimson red, the color spreading up to her ears.

"Are you sick?" he asked. "Please, don't tell me you're getting sick."

"No, I..."

"Who was that man, jiějiě?" Sile asked, more confused than angry. He reached out to pick up his tome from beyond the door when she caught his arm. He merely looked at her, waiting for her to sheepishly look away and then back to her brother.

"I don't know, but I have so many questions. Sile, introduce me!" she begged.

"I-I don't know him. He's Danbei's guest!"

"Please, Sile, walk with me then! He looks so much like..." Yinuo trailed off, her face faltering and eyes downcast. A cold enveloped her, like a reminder of the truth whispering in her ear. "I'm so stupid, little brother."

"Yinuo, what is the matter?"

"Never mind, it's stupid!"

He caught her arm, a firm expression on his face. "Fine. I'll help you."

"Sile?"

"You can't approach him on your own. Let's do it together, then. I'll bring our guests some wine to the north pavilion in an hour. Just be ready to walk past, and I'll get you your chance encounter."

"Sile! You're the best!" she cheered. She threw her arms around him and embraced him deeply before letting go.

"Yeah, yeah, stop being so clingy," he said, detaching her arms from him. He then winked at her and headed out to the main garden. Yinuo could hear him conversing with Danbei and then the gravel crunching as he made it towards the cellar.

Yinuo hurried to the north pavilion, taking cover behind a large magnolia tree beside Nainai's koi pond. Only a few white lotuses had braved the return from winter, their presence sparse amid the pond's expanse of large green pads, which offered just a narrow glimpse of her reflection. Not only did she want to look presentable, but she also wanted to rehearse what she would say. Frogs croaked nearby, and a green snake slithered its way past Yinuo without a care.

Gingerly, Yinuo sat before the pond, checking that Yaolin's efforts on her appearance hadn't been disturbed in her haste. She didn't really care about how she might appear to him; instead, she found silence in the pond, her first words unable to form with the beat of her heart. A sudden dread played its part by reminding her of the dangers of playing with 'ifs' and that the past couldn't change, but still, the overwhelming thought of possibilities lingered in her. Prince Cuilin reminded her of him.

What harm would come from just speaking with him, just for a moment? And yes, she acknowledged that maybe there would be nothing to connect Cuilin to Dehai, and she'd make as much of a fool of herself as he had with his poor proposal. But, despite the uneasiness, she had to know.

Her father's outright denial seemed almost out of character for him. He would have entertained the idea or at least not used such harsh descriptions as "caskets" and "scavengers." Yinuo patted her cheek. Nope. Of course, this would not be the suitor she married. He would be one of many who vied for her!

But he would be the only one who reminded her of Dehai.

The thought stilled her, only to be broken by Sile's laughter, causing her to snap her head towards the covered pavilion. *Okay, deep breath, a chance meeting.* She stood slowly. *This was it.* Settling her heart with gentle pats, she watched Sile and Prince Cuilin slowly coming down the path. His eyes reached for hers, a flicker of recognition flashing in his eyes, which he swiftly stifled by turning his head towards Sile, diverting his attention to answer a question she couldn't hear. *Dehai?*

Yinuo took one step before her foot caught in a root, and as ungracefully as possible, she saw herself spiraling toward the pond.

10 years prior...

Even though the gardener only ever planted them once, the peonies came back each spring to fill the space with sweetness. Looking at him curiously, Yinuo watched the gardener's son prepare a silken cushion and drape a blanket on the back of the seat with care. His blue eyes lifted to greet her with anticipation and warmth. "Here, all set!" he proclaimed. "Do you think you can transfer to it?"

"You put wheels on a chair!" she smiled brightly. "Are we going somewhere!"

"En, I have a surprise," Dehai replied, offering her his hand. She took it willingly, using him as support as she flopped into the seat to prevent putting weight on her broken leg. "Comfy?" he confirmed as she nodded. Dehai packed the blanket around her before sneaking over to the gate and sticking his head out. He put his fingers to his lips as Yinuo watched excitedly. When he was satisfied, Yinuo lifted her legs for him, and he pushed her out of the garden. He drove her past the main houses and around into an alleyway. One she never took because it was for servants, and she smiled gleefully, ready for this adventure.

No matter how much her heart thrummed, she kept her mouth shut as they approached the iron side gate. A relief of a magnolia tree and an old man sitting beneath greeted them and did not judge as Dehai shoved his shoulder into the door to open it. He leaned back all the way and struggled to get enough clearance before Yinuo pushed the wheels of the chair to escape the manor. They both cringed as the door slammed shut heavily, then turned to each other and laughed.

"Onward, Dehai!" she ordered, pointing off into the street. They rushed through the town and past the side alleyways of golden gravel, sparkling in the light, before ending up outside of the main wall and overlooking the bluffs. Rapeseed fields planted beyond the walls greeted them; fields and fields of soft puffs of yellow blanketed the rolling hills.

"It's beautiful," Yinuo whispered.

"En," Dehai replied, pushing Yinuo's chair towards it. "It's not far!"

"Take me far away, Dehai!" Yinuo proclaimed. "As far away as the Eastern Sea!"

"That's a little far," he replied. "But if you want, I'll take you as far as I can."

"Where's your imagination, Dehai?" Yinuo chided, "Okay, roll me down that hill over there! I want to play in the rapeseed!"

He complied, pushing to race the chair, occasionally taking a moment to jump on the back and let the hills propel them. The force pushed Yinuo's hair back as she squealed in glee, their speed accelerating. It bumped and jostled them from time to time before gradually rolling to a stop. Sometimes, Dehai would struggle to push her up the larger hills, but the cycle would start all over again once when they breached the summit and rolled down the next one. "Over there! Push me over to that big tree!" Yinuo ordered, and Dehai followed through.

They raced down the hill and up again, hitting a curve that sent Yinuo flying from her seat and rolling into the rapeseed. "Yinuo!" Dehai called, scared, abandoning the chair and rushing to her. Yinuo giggled, tickled by the grass, as she safely came to a stop in a dip.

She looked up between the tall grass and the yellow puffy heads to see Dehai over her with a worried expression but then a smile. She reached up to him and pulled him to her, clasping him tightly, before shoving him off and sitting up. "That was so much fun!" she proclaimed. "Dehai, do it again!"

He shook it off, his face reddening, and hand at his cheek to cover it. Dehai didn't face her; they simply looked over the scene before them. Alone in the world, two children sat between the stalks, savoring the gentle breeze that swept around them.

"Dehai," Yinuo crooned. He returned her smile and threaded his fingers through hers, giving her hand a reassuring squeeze before standing and taking a few paces away from her. Don't leave me, Yinuo thought, watching him trek back up the hill.

"Stay, Dehai," she called, and he stilled. Dehai looked over his shoulder; the faint scar on his chin, accentuated by the light, drew her focus to his smile—one she'd always remember.

Present day

He looked away. Prince Cuilin avoided her, all in the moment before a sense of shame engulfed her. With a resounding splash, the cold enveloped Yinuo as she plunged into the clear water. She reached up towards the shifting reflection and felt herself bounce as she hit the padding of mud. The motion caused billows of dirt to waft through the water. Above the pond, a blurred reflection stood, and briefly, she hoped he'd be there, when an arm latched onto hers and pulled her to the surface. Coughing and spitting out the water, Yinuo blew the stinging sensation from her nose. She rubbed at it before coming to her senses; it was freezing, and the cold spring air didn't help.

"Will she be all right?" Prince Cuilin asked, his voice distant. He hadn't even tried to save her. Yinuo snapped her head around, and saw the prince merely looking on with curiosity, still standing beside Sile. In a moment of awkwardness and empathy for his sister, Sile scratched the side of his head, averting his eyes in embarrassment.

Weixin's arm was around hers, guiding her carefully onto the gravel beside the pond to ensure she was safely out of the water before he turned to address the prince. Just then, a blue robe obscured her vision. Danni, acting swiftly, stripped off his own outer robe to drape it over her shoulders. He then positioned himself in front of her, effectively blocking her view from the others and securing the robe at the front.

"Prince Cuilin." Weixin clasped his hands together, addressing the prince.

"Is she all right?" he asked without a single inflection of his smooth voice.

"Thank you for the concern, but we, her brothers, will handle this," Weixin replied, his clothes mostly dry, except for the arm that had hoisted Yinuo from the pond. Feeling her face burn, Yinuo was then lifted to her feet by Danni, who started to march her off in the opposite direction.

"Wait," she found her words, "Wait, Danni," she pleaded with him, looking over her shoulder, desperately wishing to speak with Prince Cuilin.

Sile laughed awkwardly, throwing up the bottle, and declared, "Let's drink! Prince Cuilin, have you ever tried the General's Baijuu? He..."

Sile's voice grew softer and softer as Yinuo was pulled from the conversation. "Is it your leg? Yinuo, did you fall into the lake because of your leg?" Danni asked with urgency.

"No, I didn't. I—Let go of me, Danni!" she pushed him off her.

"Sister! Please," he blushed, looking away, "You're top..."

Looking down, Yinuo saw that her entire top had turned transparent, revealing the outline of her undershirt. Overwhelmed, she quickly squatted, pulling Danni's robe around her in an attempt to cover herself. "No, no, no," she thought, panicking before rushing off to her room. Danni followed behind, but she slammed the door in his face and flung his robe out of the side window, hiding behind a curtain. Mortified, Yinuo hit her head a few times against the side of the wall, berating herself, before she heard her brother's voice.

"Thank you for returning my zhiju!" he called. "Yinuo? Do you need me to get someone to help you dress?" Danni's voice came through the door.

"Go away, Danni!" she cried back, sinking to the floor and shaking her head. Heavens, this wasn't how she envisioned her "chance encounter" unfolding! Prince Cuilin was supposed to come rushing to her rescue, not witness her embarrassment! Frustrated with herself, Yinuo slid down against the wall. She tapped her head to the column a few more times. When she heard the door slide open, she panicked and covered herself, only to see her mother's firm presence and her maid Yaolin, arms filled with cloth, entering her room.

"Stop that," her mother ordered, snapping her fingers.

Yinuo covered her chest. "Mother, it was an accident!"

"I know it was an accident!" she snapped back.

Yinuo froze, certain she was about to get the lecture of a lifetime, when instead, her mother's panicked voice set her off balance. "You...know?"

"You would not willingly shame your family like this, Yi'er!" her mother shouted at her. She marched over and pulled her up from the floor. "You have nothing to be ashamed of. It was an accident."

"Y-Yeah," she stumbled over the words.

"Are you trying to catch your death! Yaolin, help her change," she ordered.

"Mother, I..."

"Enough," her mother said again. She dragged her over to a chair and propped up her screen as Yaolin took her behind it to help her remove the wet clothes, change her into dry linens, and retie all the ribbons. When they'd finished, Yinuo wore a plain hanfu composed of a white cross top and red skirt.

Her mother sat at the other side of the room waiting, at Yinuo's vanity, with a comb and a sour expression. She didn't say anything to her daughter but motioned for her to sit in front of her on a cushion. Yinuo slid into her place with her bad leg out in front and her other bent at the knee in front of her mother's chair.

Gently, her mother's hands reached to the sides of her long hair and let out the pins. She took a handful of her hair and, carefully in sections, began to brush it to the ends. As she combed, her mother did not say a word or even hum a tune. She simply focused on her task, with the air heavy filling the space between them, and Yinuo's heart beating in her ears.

Yinuo looked to the golden mirror on the vanity, a luxury item, her mother must have brought it in. Such an item was a privilege Yinuo rarely used, so she didn't know her own reflection. However, what else could she have expected after falling into the pond? Yaolin handed her a towel to wipe the streaking eyeliner from her face, while her mother picked at her hair.

"Aiyah," her mother sighed, "What am I supposed to do with you, Yinuo?"

"Love me?" she suggested.

"Of course, my little one," her mother sighed again. "Your father is still quite upset with you, little one, but I have spoken with him, and he's more understanding now. You did not summon Prince Cuilin, and he will not be the last of your suitors." Yinuo did not respond, waiting for her mother to finish her thoughts. "While other families are blessed with many beautiful daughters, you are my only one. So, your marriage offers a unique opportunity for others to connect with our family, namely Lord Yan's resources.

The man who marries you will gain your father's ear and expect promotions in the court or even favors from others beneath him. You know this, child. There will be leeches, snakes, and crows who all come to feed, but your father and I have known this for a long time. We should have chosen a match for you when you were younger, Yinuo."

"I wouldn't have accepted it," Yinuo murmured.

"I know, little one," she replied with a softened tone, "I know...but what happens in the past can only linger in our memories. It cannot truly come back."

Yinuo folded into herself, her head dropping to her knees as the weight of her mother's words settled around her. Her mother was right. This need to speak with Cuilin was a falsehood. She had no desire to know who or what he was, but to use him. Yinuo longed for that missing connection and the essence of Dehai near her again. Any person who could fill the role, and why not a husband? Why not someone who'd be sworn to protect her and her future? She was a fool.

Dehai is dead.

"Your father and I discussed it. Until the wedding guests have left, we're sending you to stay with my brother."

"Uncle Gao?" Yinuo asked, surprised. "Mother, if I am with Uncle, how will I help—"

"This will help," she interjected. "Uncle Gao will bring you to the wedding, and he'll bring you back after the guests have left."

"Mother, I will not—"

"Yinuo, you know better," she firmly stated.

Yinuo shook her head, "Weixin and Danni will be gone by then! And who will welcome sister-in-law!"

"The decision is final. Yaolin has already packed you. I'll dry your hair, and then you'll pick up anything else you'll need before you go. Be good for your uncle and see that you do not bother your brother Ruijian's work."

The finality in her voice made Yinuo recognize the futility of arguing with her parents. She firmed her stance and pushed off, stomping towards her bedroom, pausing for a moment before heading out towards the peony garden. She trusted Yaolin to pack her properly, but leaving was more to separate herself from her mother and avoid harsh words. Yinuo sighed when her mother's voice called from the house, "Don't wander too far! You're leaving within the hour!"

"En. En!" Yinuo dismissed. Her mother gave her space, and she found herself wandering the grounds with her head down. She had to stop doing this to herself; it was torture to remember. It was torture to hope or even wish for something so impossible. And it made her feel just as heartless, trying to replace her childhood friend with a stranger. Yinuo pouted, arms folded and head down, not really knowing where she was going.

When she looked up, she saw Dehai's form sitting and drinking like an equal with her brothers. A brief bitterness of the wholesome moment soured her disposition. The gloss from the wine on Cuilin's lips and a gentle smile led her to the scar on his chin. Violently, she shook her head. *No, don't do this, Yinuo! Don't wish.*

Form 7

Old phrases about the separation of sex be damned. Like a moth to a flame, Yinuo approached the pavilion where her brothers toasted Cuilin. The laughter echoed through her as she cautiously reached the covered platform, peeking in behind the red columns at the prince. He held his cup with one hand as her brother Sile enthusiastically downed a toast. "Gānbēi[13]!" Weixin's cheer resounded.

"Whoa, whoa, no fair, I just finished mine! Let me pour another drink!" Sile cried, almost falling over the table to pour the wine. "Okay, I'm ready."

Once more, Cuilin's smile captivated her like a lure as she took a steady breath and ascended the short stairs to join them. Around the small table, Weixin, with his back to Yinuo, sat across from Prince Cuilin, facing both the garden and Yinuo's approach. Sile positioned himself at the side of the table with his drinking bowl in hand. The table was adorned with bottles of báijiǔ, cups, and small bowls filled with dried fruits and walnuts. Curtains of red, draped around the pavilion's corners, had been tied back with ribbons that fluttered in the spring's breeze, complemented by ornate panels built into its sides that blocked the wind. There was ample space at the table, surrounded by large black cushions, to comfortably seat all her brothers.

Cuilin finished his glass, and as he went to lower it from his lips, he paused upon seeing her. "Young miss," he said, his gaze shifting to Weixin for guidance. Weixin turned his head and beckoned her to join them at the table.

"Yi'er! Are you here to toast Eldest Brother with us?" Weixin smiled.

---

[13] Drinking toast meaning "dry the cup."

"I came to say goodbye," Yinuo said. Weixin's brows furrowed, and he placed his cup down.

"Goodbye? What is this about?" he asked.

"You're leaving after the wedding, and Mother says my time is better spent outside the home," Yinuo explained, flitting her eyes to the prince.

"I see," Weixin said.

She bowed her head, hating these parting moments. "Be safe, Weixin."

"Oh, what is that?" he complained, pulling her arm down and giving her a side hug. Yinuo enveloped herself in her brother's embrace, closing her eyes and letting herself get lost in him. She opened her eyes to see him pouring her a bowl and motioning her to take it. "Drink, little sister. To the willow."

"To the willow," she replied, downing the cup as if someone had shouted gānbēi.

"What is that?" Cuilin asked softly as he topped off his glass.

"A family tradition," Weixin replied. "Yinuo, you've met Prince Cuilin officially now, right?"

Yinuo nodded and turned to him. "We have been introduced. You are Lord Nie's adopted son?"

"En, close enough. He is my uncle. I am a prince of Zhou."

"I have...scarcely heard of that place," she replied.

"It does not surprise me; as long as I stay, Zhou remains a name on our maps. Happily forgotten and out of conflict."

"It must be hard to be so far from home," she stated.

"En," he dismissed, glancing away and taking his drink to avoid her.

She turned to her brother and explained, "Weixin, I can't stay and keep you company. Mother expects me to pack for Uncle Gao's place."

"Will I see you at the ceremony?" Cuilin asked.

Yinuo paused, then chided herself internally. She nodded and said simply, "I wouldn't miss it. It's the first time in a long time we've had a reason for all my brothers to come together."

"It's good to have family," he replied.

"Tell me about yours," she asked, not thinking if bringing up family might upset him.

The prince smirked but let the comment go. "My uncle takes good care of me," he said, inclining his head—a polite response, but closed the subject. Yinuo leaned forward, elbows on the table, again taking in his face. Perhaps she was mistaken; Dehai did not have the large scar that traversed the left side, beginning at his brow, slashing across his eyes, and ending at his upper cheek—only the small one that graced his chin.

"Yinuo," Sile whispered, "It's rude to stare."

"Ah, let her stare," Weixin waved off, his cheeks flushed, taking his bottle and pouring another bowl. "Prince Cuilin, shall I pour you another?"

"Please," he said.

"Gēgē, Danni gē is going to be mad at you if you finish the bottle without him."

"Danni doesn't need to know," Weixin shushed him.

"He said he's coming back!" protested Sile. "Pour mine, too!" he added excitedly as the last drop of liquid filled his cup. Yinuo had finished her báijiǔ and merely shook her head.

"Would you like mine?" Cuilin offered.

"No, it wouldn't be proper."

"Rules." Cuilin rolled his eyes. "Weixin, we've run out of wine."

"Youngest! Go get the good stuff!" Weixin declared.

Sile soured at the notion, but obediently smiled as he finished the last of his drink and pushed off of the table. As Sile went to fetch another bottle, his movements lively and his demeanor gleeful, Yinuo watched him with interest. Meanwhile, Weixin released his arm from around his sister and took another sip of his drink. "Ah...gotta slow down. Sorry, Yinuo."

"It's fine," she said, "When was the last time you enjoyed drinking?"

"After the archery game," he commented after a slight delay, prompting Yinuo to wonder how much wine her brother had indulged in, though she refrained from voicing her concern. Her brother continued, "That's when Danbei and I finished off General Lei's báijiǔ. Though he sent another bottle, and that's what we're having now."

"Danbei gave you the general's gift?"

"He's sharing them. Danbei's received at least a few cases of fine báijiǔ. We're not going to finish them before the end of the wedding."

"He's very generous," Yinuo said.

"Poor General Lei, he doesn't realize that Danbei only politely drinks when his brother asks him," Weixin said. Yinuo felt his forehead with the back of her hand.

"Don't drink so much, brother. Savour it."

"You sound like Danni," he protested, sipping his drink and closing his eyes. Ever the general—except for his cheeks; they were pink and felt good against her skin. Her brother rarely permitted himself such enjoyment. Here at home, it was a good place to find some freedom.

"What do I have to do to earn that smile?" Cuilin whispered.

"Excuse me?" Yinuo turned to him, carefully lowering her hand.

"I-um," Prince Cuilin averted his eyes, his own cheeks coloring. "You weren't supposed to hear that," he murmured.

Don't do this, Yinuo, she told herself. Get up and walk away now before he hurts your heart. Before you grow attached to him. "I should really get going. I'm sorry for staring at your scars and if I made you self-conscious."

"Wait, please stay. I wouldn't mind."

"I should go," Yinuo said, offering a half-smile. "Weixin will have another round with you, my prince, if he doesn't fall asleep before then."

"Please stay," he whispered.

Yinuo glimpsed at her brother, who appeared sound asleep, his arm propped gently on his knee. Whether he was pretending or not, she couldn't tell, but his breaths were even. This would be the most alone she could be with Prince Cuilin. A moment was all she needed to confirm if he was Dehai, but being here, Yinuo couldn't make the decision. She thought she was ready, but didn't want to know the pain the truth would have.

"Prince Cuilin," Yinuo began, casting her eyes down. Folding her hands properly in front of her and avoiding his sky eyes, she spoke to him. "Be honest with me. Why did your father propose marriage before it was appropriate?"

There was a pause, and then another; Yinuo lifted her eyes to his, searching for truth when she only saw hesitation. She shook her head and said, "You don't want to marry me. My heart is as withered as a peony, its decaying heads too transient to make an impact." She rose from kneeling, but abruptly stopped.

Weixin grabbed her arm, tugging her down to her knees again, "Wait, mèimei," he ordered. Looking up through the haze, her brother shook his head and stretched. He tilted his cup and looked at it solemnly. "It would be rude to leave before the round is finished."

"The round is finished, brother. Sile went to get a new bottle."

Weixin scrunched up his face and then flopped back on his cushion, facing the ceiling. "I'm going to nap until he gets here. Keep the prince company," he mumbled, then promptly drifted off once more.

"Weixin?" Yinuo's plea went unheard. She then turned to her empty cup with an awkward smile. "I..."

"Don't wake him," Cuilin said.

Yinuo hesitated, her lips parting slightly as she glanced up again. "I..." but she stopped herself. Without prompting, Cuilin stood, his movements slow and deliberate. There was no limp, but she recognized the struggle in his body language. Whatever he suffered, pain or even fatigue, the prince carried himself with a regal grace. He didn't even grimace, but Yinuo saw, or more, she felt it as she observed his body language. Leaning on the rail behind him momentarily, Prince Cuilin took careful steps past her and the sleeping Weixin, pausing only when he reached the stairs.

"Is it me?" he said softly, "Is my title as' hostage prince' making you uncomfortable?"

"It is not that," she replied without bothering to face him. Yinuo stood, gave a bob, and stepped past the steps. She skipped the last one and was on her way when she felt a slight tug at the back of her sleeve. Looking, Prince Cuilin had her jacket pinched between his fingers in a last attempt to keep her.

"You're going to get me in trouble," she whispered.

Cuilin stayed his hands, a look of defeat on his face. "This isn't how I imagined things going."

"Did you imagine my father would agree?"

"I merely wished to be the first to express my interest."

Caught by him, Yinuo tried to form the prince into the boy from her memory, but even if she could, it was hard to picture it all in her head. What changes would the boy have gone through to look like the man before her? She wanted him to fit the mold, but it hurt, too. It hurt to look upon him and pretend that her friend was standing in front of her. Suddenly, all Yinuo wanted was for him to let go.

It must have shown in her face, because he recoiled his hand and brought it to cover the slight blush at his scarred cheek. "Are you—"she stopped herself, "Who are you?"

"Prince...Cuilin of Zhou," he stated, a coldness seeping into his words. Almost to the point that Yinuo didn't believe him.

"In the future, please do not be so forward. It places us both in an awkward position." Her heart beat at her, almost in protest of her intense tones. She bit her lip and forced herself away from him, breaking into a run as she battled her urge to apologize. Why? What did she have to apologize for? She wasn't the one crossing boundaries. One moment, he felt so indifferent, and the next, he made her feel foolish.

Meanwhile, Prince Cuilin's eyes never left her, even when she passed the corner and exited the northern pavilion. Abruptly, Weixin sat up and brushed his cheek. He let out an audible sigh. "What am I going to do with you, friend?" he asked. The only alcohol left in his cup was barely residue of the sweet liquor. Weixin dipped his tongue into the rim and licked the last sharp drop. Rising to his full height, he placed a hand on his friend's shoulder, shaking his head in disappointment. "You lost your chance, friend."

"I'll find another one," he responded quietly as if the desire wasn't permitted of him.

"Don't hesitate next time," Weixin advised before removing his hand from Cuilin's shoulder and walking off the steps.

"I have to find another one," Prince Cuilin whispered; the urgency in his voice bore at desperation, leaving Weixin to raise an eyebrow and catch his neck from turning. He returned his focus forward instead of addressing the prince. Weixin knew his intentions were pure, even if it seemed Cuilin was on the path to doing something very foolish.

Double Happiness

8

Before she left her home, Danni prepared her one last talisman for a safe journey. While Yinuo appreciated the gesture, she initially resisted taking the token before he pressed it into her hands and said even if the journey wasn't far, she still deserved protection on the road. Uncle Gao's house sat at the edge of the town, within walking distance, but her brother Ruijian met her at the gate with a carriage while her father looked on as if just another task were being completed.

That was two days ago; today, she woke up beside her cousin Taomei, wheezing in her sleep, the only reprieve she got from the blabbermouth. Don't misplace her affection; Yinuo loved her cousin and brushed a strand of hair from Taomei's mouth. She'd always wanted a sister, but each pregnancy her mother borne had been a boy; first Ruijian, then Mingdan, Sile, and even the one they buried had been male. Her parents must have done many good deeds in their past lives to have had so many sons.

And it bothered her slightly that she had this desire to connect with Danbei's bride, Lei Xing, knowing full well that after her own marriage, she would probably see the woman once a year. Daughters are like water; they disappear. At least, that's what Nainai said, and she'd had six sisters and one brother.

With that unpleasant thought, she quickly got ready for the morning. Eager to get to Lei Xing's house to meet her mother and help her future sister-in-law dress. She was excited, bustling even, grabbing a pomegranate from the bowl of fruit on the table. Carefully packing up some final supplies, she made her way towards the main gate. The sun hadn't risen in the sky, and overcast clouds lingered around them. A storm was coming, and she ignored the twinge in her leg.

"Miss, where are you going?" a maid called to her, carrying a vase.

"I need to meet my mother at General Lei's. Where is the carriage?" she explained.

The woman cocked her head and then shook it. "There were no instructions about leaving so early. Please, go back to bed. Master Gao is not expected at the wedding until the afternoon."

"I have to go! I can't miss my brother's wedding! I have to help—"

"Yi'er," her uncle's grim voice called from the main house, still with sleep in his eyes.

"Uncle! Have them prepare me a carriage. I have to meet—"

"No," he stated in an obsolete tone that stunned Yinuo as if she had been struck. "We are not leaving, and you are excused from the familial obligations, child."

"Uncle!"

"What is this disrespect!"

"Has Ruijian left! My family would not exclude me from this important role."

"Your mother asked me to protect you. You're staying on the grounds until we leave," he ordered. A guard grabbed her arm, and she yanked herself free of him.

"How dare you," she retorted at him. "Uncle, please," she begged him.

"Bring her back to Taomei's room," he ordered again, brushing her off and returning to his room. Every instinct told her to run, but instead, a flurry of pink lunged at her, catching her arm. Taomei's pleading eyes grasped her shoulders.

"Come, jiějiě! We'll have breakfast together!" Taomei said urgently, looking towards the guards. "No need to be rough with her. I'll make sure she doesn't leave."

"What is this about Taomei?" Yinuo asked.

She pressed her finger to Yinuo's lips, "Sh." Taomei dragged her back to her room, and as the door slid shut, two shadows guarded them.

"What is going on?" she asked.

"Father has the best intentions, jiějiě!" Taomei said.

"What do you know, Taomei?" Yinuo leaned into her. One of the perks of her being a gossip meant that she couldn't keep a secret either. Yinuo leaned in as Taomei's face flitted with expressions from resistance to smugness. All Yinuo had to do was slightly cant her head.

"Okay! Okay! There were more suitors!" she bleated. "A servant said they saw someone stalking you, and they didn't want you to worry!"

"What! That's ridiculous. I spend my life at home; who would be stalking me?" she probed to get the name of the entity. However, her family's fears didn't reflect her feelings towards the peaceful entity that only made her aware it watched her. Yinuo folded her arms and shook her head.

"It's true! Jiějiě!" Taomei pleaded. "There are all sorts of rumors, and I think the hostage prince has the most vile intent! They say he's vying for a political marriage to appease the Emperor, and last week, a maid died from touching a half-written hex in his room!"

"You shouldn't listen to such nonsense, Taomei," Yinuo said. "I don't care about the rumors. I am going to be a part of my brother's wedding. I am going to make a connection with my sister-in-law."

"Jiějiě? Aren't you terrified that someone could have ill intent because your father holds an important role in the court! What if someone is hiding among the guests to abduct or hurt you! The wedding will have so many strangers."

"And all my family to protect me," Yinuo stomped her foot. "If they dare to interrupt a wedding, heaven will not turn a blind eye." Yinuo shook her head. "Mèimei, I won't be scared. My family is too important to me to be scared."

Taomei sighed, but did not say anything else. It wasn't until the afternoon that her uncle decided it was time for them to leave. Taomei hadn't finished putting on her makeup, and Yinuo helped her in the carriage to avoid mistakes with the bumpy ride. The rain hadn't come yet, but the gloom falling over them continued to approach. Taomei squeezed her hand with a reassuring smile as the carriage came to a crawl, and she jumped out in front of Yan Estate.

Yinuo climbed down, catching herself on the side, as her leg again refused to function. She smacked it gently. "Yinuo!" Danbei called to her, and she looked up to him dressed in fine red silk.

"Congratulations, Danbei. How was the parade?"

"Perfect. Is your leg okay?"

"I'm fine; don't fuss over me!" she called back. A servant passed her the bundle of silks, and she thanked her before turning to her brother, who was busy engaging with her uncle and Taomei. Yinuo dipped away from the greeting party, passing her family and guests with smiles and purpose as she slipped into the room where her future sister-in-law had been set up. A gaggle of women surrounded a central figure, blocking Yinuo from her. She cleared her throat, and her mother, at the center, turned to see her.

"Yinuo," she said simply, "Come greet your sister."

The small framed woman behind her sat in a chair, dressed in a beautiful hanfu of red and greens. Mouselike, almost to the point of not looking at her. Yinuo gave her best smile as she drew near. "My name is Yan Yinuo, I am your—"

"Little sister," Lei Xing corrected, "It is nice to put a face to the name."

"Y-yes, congratulations on your marriage," she said. "I..umm..."

"Yinuo?" her mother prompted, and she held out the bundle.

"I prepared some silks to make gowns for infants. I hope they're to your liking," she smiled. A maid at Lei Xing side, possibly with her since childhood, took them from her and then presented them to Lei Xing. In return, her sister smiled gently but did not thank her or comment on them.

"My lady, the wedding should start soon," her maid interrupted the silence, tucking away her silks. Yinuo's mother took her elbow and stationed her to the side as she switched places with her.

Never had Yinuo felt so detached. Set to the side like everything she had done to get the silks had been for nothing. Yinuo closed her mouth and remained silent to the other women who continued to fuss over Lei Xing. She got lost in the background of their laughter. Yinuo wasn't a part of this, she was a part.

Feeling dejected, Yinuo slipped into the main hall and brushed her dry face. Suddenly, the pain in her leg intensified, a persistent ache that had been haunting her all day. The rain hadn't broken from the sky yet, but it would rain on her brother's wedding day. The daunting thought of having to smile made her grimace a little more.

"You'll sour the occasion with a face like that," a voice called to her, prompting Yinuo to throw down her hands and turn to meet the speaker. She found herself facing dark, intense eyes, but a smiling disposition nonetheless. Well dressed in robes fitting for the ceremony, his eyes lingered over her form. "I take it my sister has offended you. She's not easily impressed, but your gesture is surely appreciated."

Yinuo bit her tongue, finally appreciating the custom of not speaking to strange men. Though, from the way he carried himself and the sound of his voice, she figured that this man was associated with the Lei family. You couldn't hide his rigorous posture, or the way that his steel eyes evaluated every inch of her presence like a general surveying troops. The man smiled, coyly brushing his hair from his face and tucking it behind his ear.

He continued to speak, "I am surprised. I have heard that the Yan's daughter is known for her boldness. I hope I haven't offended you by speaking without an introduction. Let me remedy this," he bowed to her, with a grace she had only ever known in the courts. "I am Lei Yingzhe, the bride's brother."

Yinuo did not reply. She knew the origin of his gaze. The ominous feeling she experienced was as if she were greeting a beast instead of a man. This was the "family friend," the intruder who had inquired about Dehai. She bit her tongue.

"Well?" he raised his eyes to her.

"Yinuo!" Weixin's voice boomed from behind her. She gave a bob and ran to join her brother.

"Ah, Master Weixin, it has been a while since we last met. You seem concerned. I was merely inquiring about your sister's wellbeing. The weather looks as if it will turn soon."

"We are needed in the grand hall for the ceremony," Weixin stressed, taking his arm around her shoulder. "Lei," he dismissed him. Yinuo turned with her brother, following him into the hall as the uncomfortable feeling lingered on her back. She was glad for Weixin's arm, and felt sad when it left her. She took her place away from Lei Yingzhe, but could not escape his eyes. They lined up in birth order at the side of the wedding spar for Danni, who was performing rites, so she stood between Weixin and Ruijian.

As the ceremony progressed, with Danbei and Lei Xing walking towards their parents and familial shrines, Yinuo thought they balanced each other. However, after that, she lost most of the experience, distracted with the thoughts in her head. She heard "bow to heaven" and "bow to parents," but everything else started to blur.

Because her uncle wouldn't take her to General Lei's, she'd missed helping Lei Xing dress and quelling her qualms about marriage—the sisterly things she had desired ever since learning she would finally have a sister. Yet, the pang that ate at her more was the family breakfast she should have been at. When would be the next time she ate with Danni or Weixin as a family? Why was she so isolated from the people she wanted to be with the most?

Ruijian took her hand. "Are you all right," he whispered. Yinuo nodded but then felt him wipe her tears from the side of her face. Out of all her brothers, Ruijian was the most reliable. He pulled a handkerchief from his shirt and passed it to her.

"It's just beautiful," she lied, brushing off the tears, and then thanked him silently.

Weixin pulled her into a side hug with a whisper in her ear. "You're okay."

Yinuo nodded. The ceremony finished with cheers and hollers of joy around her. Then they followed the bride and groom out into the courtyard where the banquet was being held. Weixin didn't release her until they'd reached partway, and he saw friends who beckoned him to drink.

A maid hurried over to her as soon as he'd parted from her. "Young Miss, please help! There's an urgent issue with one of the dishes! We need your advice right away!"

"Yes," she said, her excitement almost too much. "Of course, how can I help?"

"It's Lady Xi! She's having an allergic reaction to the bitter melon mango slaw! We didn't know, young miss!"

"Take me to her," she quickly instructed the servant, then followed them to one of Lei's elderly relatives, fanning herself with swollen lips.

"Oh, Madame! I am so sorry about this," Yinuo stepped forward. "How can I help?"

"Aiyah! This is nothing! Who said to make such a fuss? I will be fine after a minute. I am just thankful my Xiao Mei saw the dreaded fruit before I'd taken more of a bite!"

"Stay with Madame Xi. I will be back in a moment," Yinuo bobbed, then hurried to the kitchen. She grabbed another servant, pulling her aside. "Lady Xi is allergic to mangoes; please ensure her tables have something else. There's fresh star fruit we can serve instead. The meat isn't prepared with a mango glaze, is it?"

"No, young miss, braised duck with goji berries is set to be served," the cook replied.

"Good, hand me that fine china, and follow me with a bottle of huángjiǔ. I'll get this settled." Yinuo helped to cut up star fruit and arranged them with a simple syrup over the edges. She cleaned the bowl and smiled at the refined elegance before rushing back to Lady Xi.

"Ah, young miss! What do I owe the pleasure?" Lady Xi said happily.

"Here, Madame, fresh star fruit with simple syrup. It will be a wonderful appetizer to the braised ducks the chefs have prepared. And here," she motioned for the servant to bring her finest porcelain cup set. "A toast to the lovely bride. Have a drink with me, grandmother."

"Ah, I have inherited a capable granddaughter! See, Jingjing, Young Miss Yan, is a capable host. Her mother is lucky to have her to help." Yinuo drank with the women at the table, mending the relationship as quickly as it had been severed with mangoes. She smiled happily, the crisis averted. "Tell me, Miss Yan, when will you be celebrating your wedding? I would love to return this kind gesture."

"So many are eager to see me married, my brother has barely had an hour of happiness," Yinuo expressed.

"We've heard there have been several proposals. Jingjing, your husband mentioned Lord Yan's dismay at the list of prospects just yesterday, correct?"

"En, Miss Yan, has your father not shared it with you?" she inquired, the woman's cheeks rosy from wine.

"The wedding preparations must have delayed him. I only knew of the one from Lord Nie, though my father said he wouldn't entertain any prospects until after today."

"Oh, that Nie!" the woman spat. "Yinuo, dear, do not even consider him. Prince Cuilin is nothing but trouble for a young woman! He will break your heart and ruin your reputation! Have you not heard of him?"

"Oh, Jiaoqi, don't bring this up on a happy day," Jingjing protested. "But...if we were to warn the young miss. We do not wish to see a bright young woman suffer from the misled affections of a hostage prince."

"Prince Cuilin has already angered the Emperor and put his delicate position in danger. He escaped the palace once before, and as punishment for trying to leave, he was put out into the front lines."

"En. That is why he's so frightful. The coward was captured and had to be rescued, but not before the enemy scarred him. He nearly lost his eye in the battle."

"Exactly!" the woman said as she poured herself another cupful. "Young Yinuo, no matter what your father says, you cannot even bring yourself close to that man! "

"Lady Yinuo would look better at Young Master Lei's side," the elderly Jingjing giggled.

"Oh, what a lovely pair that'd be!" Madame Xi boasted. "He is such a just and handsome man!" the woman shook her head, prompting her maid to pour her wine again.

"Have you no compassion!" Yinuo snapped at them, rising to her feet as her hands slammed onto the table. She could only see the smug faces of the women before her, oblivious to the curious stares from onlookers. "He almost lost his life, and he risked everything, only to be treated so horribly!" Yinuo keenly felt the pain of being trapped and the lack of control in her own life. "How can you mock him!"

A clap of thunder broke her retort, and screams erupted as a torrent of rain filled the courtyard. The women panicked and rushed toward the main hall, while Yinuo seized the moment to escape from her new relatives. Rain poured down in buckets, soaking her to the bone and blurring her vision with its swirling colors as servants struggled to bring in the plates. It was as if the weather had finally broken, mirroring the disquieted storm within her, the last straw of her composure swept away in the downpour.

Her leg seized up, and she stumbled, caught by a flailing hand through the storm. The blurred image of a man dragged her from the courtyard and rushed her toward the back gardens. She recognized the smudged peonies and then the latticework on the covered pavilion as the man brought her to the center and placed her on a rosewood chair. The rain was relentless, pounding against the shelter but not invading the space.

In a sweeping motion, the man shed his outer robe, the fabric flowing gracefully before he deftly draped it over the rail. As he turned towards her, drops of rain clung to his dark hair, like morning dew on fresh blossoms. His piercing blue eyes met hers, capturing her breath in their intense gaze. A subtle scent of earth and rain mingled with the delicate fragrance of peony, stilling her world.

Earth, rain, and peonies all invaded the moment their eyes met again. Her heart tapped at the base of her throat, resisting the urge to reach out—to call out, and still, she did not do any of these things. Sitting in the edging cold that tapered around her wrist and neckline, her cheeks burned against the chill.

"Prince Cuilin?" she whispered.

"Are you all right now?" he asked, lifting his eyes to her. She nodded her head slowly, taking him in for another moment. Tracing the strands of hair that clung to the contours of his cheek and chin with her gaze, she felt a surge of tenderness. Yinuo would take a thousand moments with him, even if the truth broke the dream. He wiped the slick from his hair and smiled softly towards her as he approached. "I'm glad you're okay."

Again, she nodded.

"Are you angry with me?" he asked her. She shook her head. "Then please, speak openly with me."

"I'm not angry," she spoke up, "I just don't know what to say. I feel as if I have learned something deeply personal, and it wasn't my right to know."

He touched his cheek. "This scar, you mean?"

"I apologize, I didn't mean to make you—"

"Stop," he replied quietly. "You don't make me uncomfortable, and I know you have good intent." Before speaking again, Prince Cuilin closed his fist and eyes to take a breath. "Those women were right. You shouldn't jeopardize your reputation by defending me. Please refrain from doing so—"

A crash of thunder boomed. "I will not!" Yinuo shouted. "Those women had no right makes those horrendous claims. They treated you like you weren't a person and made assumption of your character based on a life they have never lived! What if you were their son? Trapped in another world away from everything and everyone who has ever loved you? They would not bare an ounce of that pain! They are fat and spoiled, and I am ashamed on them. I couldn't let them continue! You are a person and deserve to be treated like such with compassion!"

He stilled. "Miss Yan."

"I will defend anyone who is treated so miserably. It sickens me to my core that I even have a connection to them now. I don't know your story, my prince, but it cannot be easy to live so far from home and have so much expected of you. So, I decline. Let me worry about my own reputation, I will say what I want to whom I want."

"You're too kind to me," he awed. "Your act of kindness should not go unrewarded, but I am afraid that I do not have the assets to properly do so. If I were home, gold and precious jade would be finer, but as I have none..." he walked towards the garden, kneeling at the peonies.

Yinuo tilted her head, her eyes catching the glint of a concealed knife within his sleeve. With practiced ease, he deftly selected and clipped a stem from the bush, meticulously removing the leaves with a few skilled twists. Rising with grace, he discreetly tucked the knife away and moved out of the rain's embrace. Approaching her, he knelt by her chair and revealed the perfectly prepared red peony from behind his back.

Misted in dew, fragrantly sweet, the sudden crash of thunder caused her to spring to her feet, covering her ears involuntarily. "Take it," he whispered, unphased by the loud, resounding boom of thunder or the crack of lightning so close. Alone in the torrent, Yinuo's heart thrummed at the base of her neck. It cannot be. Slowly, she reached towards his cheek, drawing him close to her and pressing her lips to his soft ones. The warmth of his breath heats her own as she invades his space and lifts him towards her. A hand caresses her back, tracing her spine with gentle pressure as the peony lies lifelessly on the ground.

Caught in the softness, the dance of pressure and heat. The warmth that flushes her face and the base of her neck. She pulled up for air and found more of him ready and eager to hold her close to his icy form. A sweetness of flowers and musk at his skin, pulling her close and in. It felt right.

It felt like it should be. The other part of her heart beating in his chest pressed to hers. Instead of pulling away, she wanted more; he wanted more than the gentle taps of the rain on the roof. She knew this man. She knew every caress, every feel of his lips against hers. She'd tasted him before, like maltose sweets.

She broke her latest kiss, cupping his face and searching his eyes once more. Whoever he was, she was his, and he hers, and in the rain, she vowed she'd never lose him again. "Cuilin," she whispered.

He did not respond to the name, but he did not pull back from her either, captured in an embrace intimate and forbidden. It did not matter to the couple, whose whole world was only rain and each other. Yinuo shook her head. "I know you," she crooned.

He nodded, "I—"

"What is the meaning of this!" shouted a blurred image rapidly approaching the pavilion. Anxiety spiraled within Yinuo, her hold on him tightening as fear overwhelmed her.

"Run!" Yinuo implored, shoving against Prince Cuilin with all her might. "Please, run! Don't let them take you—not again, Dehai!"

He firmed his stance, gripping her hand. "I will not run."

"No, not like this! Go, you fool!" she pleaded, her voice cracking. She ripped herself away from him, only for her leg to betray her, sending her tumbling to the ground.

"Yinuo!" he shouted, reaching out and catching her arm—a loud tear screeched through the air. Yinuo clutched her shoulder, knocked to her knees. Her chest lay exposed, and her sleeve torn. The shadows that breached the entrance of the pavilion froze as dread captured Prince Cuilin's face.

"What is the meaning of this!" Lei Yingzhe hissed! "Miss Yan, are you all right!"

"I am—"

"How dare you attack her!" he shouted, "Under my authority as the Minister of Justice, I am compelled to detain you, Prince Cuilin of Zhou!"

"No!" Yinuo cried.

"Take me to Lord Yan," Cuilin demanded, standing between him and Yinuo. She attempted to hoist herself up using the chair, but lost her grip on the smooth surface and stumbled.

"Ah!" she exclaimed, her hand smacking hard against the floor.

"Are you all right?" Prince Cuilin's head swiveled.

"What are you waiting for! Arrest the prince!" Lei Yingzhe demanded. Two of the wedding guests pushed forward, latching onto Cuilin's arm. He resisted, yanking his arm free.

"Let me see that she's all right!"

"She is not your concern! Take him away! Find her maid; don't just stand there! Can't you see she's indecent!" Lei Yingzhe shouted.

"This is all a misunderstanding!" Yinuo cried. She pushed through Lei Yingzhe and bullied her way in front. "Don't do this, Young Master Lei! He is not—"

"That is Magistrate Lei," he interjected.

"Arrest me too! I—"

"You are distraught; for heaven's sake, bring someone to take care of Young Miss Yan!" he bellowed. A strange woman grabbed her upper arm to prevent her from approaching.

"No! Prince Cuilin!" she cried.

"Yinuo, it wasn't your fault!" he called. "None of this is your fault, Yinuo!" Prince Cuilin stressed as the men pushed him away, followed by Lei Yingzhe, who gave her a disgusted look before turning his attention back to the prince.

How? How could he say that? Yinuo contemplated internally. *It'd been her fault. Everything had been her fault.* She pressed the uncomfortable feeling down, but vividly heard and saw her memories interrupting the moment.

"Here," Dehai cooed. Holding out the delicate pink peony to her youthful self. Her leg pain only a faint reminder of the weeks he'd spent nursing her back to health. Of all the moments where she searched for his smile and played with him in the garden, Yinuo cherished this one the most. The whole world was bright, it lingered in the corner of his smile, and made the adult standing vigilant feel every weight of the innocence.

It mocked her with each lash that crashed against his skin. Yinuo bit into the flesh of her lips, regretting every moment, every stolen kiss, every 'I like you, Dehai.' She would take it all back if it meant she could watch him quietly grow. Quietly marry another. Quietly linger over her form.

Yinuo couldn't hear the words from the woman besides her, whether they were meant in comfort or concern with her ripped sleeve. She focused on the back of Prince Cuilin and how the blurring rain stole her from him.

Dehai had been the same, swallowed by a storm on another day. Tears threatened her eyes, but even though the adult did not cry, her inner child wept in a screeching pain. It reached for Prince Cuilin, clinging to his shirt, begging for him. "Dehai is dead," she whispered to herself. You cannot have him back. You cannot have so much hope, Yinuo. She chided herself, feeling the tears even though she did not shed a single one.

In that moment, shadowed by her inner child, she was guided back to her deepest regret—a peony. The air was warm, the spring breeze gentle, swaying the cherry blossoms and wafting the scent of chūnbǐng[14] through the air. Her Dehai had only dirt beneath his nails, yet the delicate and expertly prepared peony became her source of warmth. "Here," he whispered, his cheek flushed and awkward. A joy sprouted from her impulsiveness, and in response, she pulled him to her lips, kissing him as a child does—quickly and briefly, without deeper meaning or intent.

---

[14] A thin Chinese pancake often enjoyed in springtime.

"I like you, Dehai. I will always like you," she confessed, her cheeks burning and beaming in his presence. He turned his eyes away, but his hand reached out to her to clutch tightly. She wanted to stay in the warmth, but a rustle of leaves betrayed her. Yinuo always denied she knew which brother had informed her father, but each tap of his retreating footstep stabbed her heart, sealing it with the betrayal she could never amend.

She recoiled her hand too late.

She denied her father too late.

She protested too late.

Yinuo grasped her ears, but she could still hear the lash, see the bruises, and watch in horror as her brother held her to his placket to prevent her from seeing her family's punishment. A servant crossed the line, his father was flogged along with him and expelled from the household.

And she was left to kneel in the mud, bearing the agony of her bent leg, not yet fully healed from the break. Yinuo spent hours in the garden. The rain unleashed a torrent of storms around her, yet she could still hear him screaming. What else could she do but call out to drown out the noise, the torrent taking all her senses?

"I kissed him," she whispered. "Don't hurt him anymore. Don't! Let him go. I did it. I hurt him. I kissed him. Please, Father! Big brother! I am the one—" A hand rasped against her face, a streak she still felt from the signet ring at her cheek.

Yinuo traced it with her fingertips, brought back to the present by the aunt trying to maneuver her away. She broke free, shoving the person away from herself and running towards the great hall. Rain impeded her steps, and pain lingered in her bad leg. No! She wouldn't be late this time. She wouldn't be blind to the consequences of her affection. She made a promise when she kissed him.

Hesitation

10

Inside the great hall, droves of guests filled each crevice, celebrating the marriage with cheers and alcohol that clinked and disoriented Yinuo. Panic rising in her heart, she bolstered her way through the guests—some gasping at her torn sleeve, others crying out for her to stop and join them. She couldn't, though, not when Cuilin could be harmed because of her recklessness. Yinuo had escaped her aunt and now ignored each cry, carrying herself tall and looking for her father and Prince Cuilin. He wasn't there. She ducked beneath a large round serving tray and rushed her way towards the back of the hall.

"Miss Yan!" someone called for her, but she didn't hear them. Moving without thought, she dodged under a table to lose herself into the crowd and emerged on the other side of the hall. They must have taken him to her father's study. It would be the only secluded place in the wedding, and she found the doors shut, but a light came from beyond.

Yinuo steeled her heart, shoving herself through the sliding door just as a resounding slap echoed across the room. "How dare you lay a single finger on my daughter! I will have them broken one by one!" her father shouted.

"Father!" she screamed, seeing that his hand had struck the prince. "Stop this at once!" She rushed them, inserting herself between her father and Prince Cuilin. Besides her father, a chorus of the court, old ministers and officials who were friends of the family, looked on at the scene as if they were judges of the crime. Their faces were red from the drink, and their eyes were glossy, with a disturbed irritation from being taken away from the ceremony. Some stood with raised hands to cover their whispers, their efforts made evident by the flickering light of the dimmed candles. The light turned them into shades, hooding their eyes and making the whole assembly feel as if darker in intent.

Lord Nie prostrated himself in front of the court and her father's desk, a symbol of his authority, while a guard looked on without the need to lay a hand on Lord Nie for their intent to be made clear. Families fell for the actions of one; Yinuo dreaded this as the frail man did nothing in response to Cuilin's treatment. Whatever Yinuo had interrupted, even Lord Nie didn't believe in his innocence. A bitterness coated her throat as she stole a glance at Cuilin, whose arms were restrained behind his back by two palace guardsmen.

Besides them, Lei Yingzhe looked smug and then marred by her sudden appearance.

"How dare—Yinuo! What are you doing here!" her father demanded from her.

"How dare you!" she retorted, "Release him this instant, and let me explain! Magistrate Lei is jumping to conclusions and doesn't understand the situation!"

"Magistrate Lei would not make such light accusations! Besides, look at yourself, daughter! Your ruqun is clearly torn!" Lord Yan's voice boomed, his eyes sweeping critically over the tear on her sleeve.

"Because I fell! He was merely trying to help me up!"

"You are too ignorant to know of a man's true intentions! You shouldn't have been alone with him in the first place!"

"He never hurt me!"

"You do not know what has happened! He will be made responsible for his actions!"

"Tell me then! Tell me his crimes if I am so ignorant of them! I am the victim here! Shouldn't I be the one to scream to the heavens my wrong! I have none to scream!"

"And still, our voices are raised!"

"You won't listen to me!" she retorted, aiming to strike her father.

"That is enough," Prince Cuilin's growl cut through the crowd, freezing Yinuo in her step. As if she'd fallen into a frozen lake, the stinging sensation hit her. A calm fell over the room as Yinuo distanced herself from her father and Prince Cuilin. He glared to the two men restraining him and then addressed Yinuo with a restrained head bow. "I am—"

"Don't," Yinuo interrupted him, fear racing her heart. She shook her head.

"Let me finish," he said.

Yinuo bit the bottom of her lip. No, she couldn't have him be her shield; she couldn't bear the thought of him taking responsibility for her actions. "There's been a misunderstanding. Please, Father, hear me out. You know, I would never knowingly shame my family or myself. Prince Cuilin—"

"I have heard enough," he spat, turning away from her and towards Magistrate Lei. He opened his mouth when a resounding voice replaced his.

"But not all of the truth," a voice boomed from behind them. Sweat glistened across Danbei's brow as he pulled the door open and stood there, almost panting with a slight disarray look to his wedding red hanfu. The tone sounded just like their father's, as it silenced the entire room. Danbei handed an umbrella to a nearby servant and marched himself up down the aisle and towards the others.

With the proper bow, Danbei raised his eyes to his father and challenged the authority in the whole of the room. "What are you doing here?" Yinuo whispered, but Danbei ignored her comment.

"Magistrate Lei's report of the crime, while done so with good intent, has been misguided," he proclaimed.

"You have evidence of otherwise; bring it forward, Young Master Yan," Magistrate Lei responded with an incline of his head.

Danbei nodded and then said, "I serve as evidence and a witness to the events that unfolded. Prince Cuilin did not assault my sister, nor did he engage in any form of questionable misconduct with her. As the rains began to pour, Yinuo, like many other guests, sought shelter. Observing her struggle in the open, made vulnerable by the storm due to her weakened leg, Prince Cuilin acted out of concern. My Lords, Magistrate Lei, it's known that Yinuo suffered a leg injury in her youth, an ailment that never fully healed. While she bears this quietly, it pains her significantly, especially during storms.

Had Prince Cuilin not intervened, Yinuo might have remained exposed to the storm, risking injury or worse. My brothers and I, while securing furniture against the storm's wrath, witnessed their attempt to find cover under the pavilion. Startled by a clap of thunder, Yinuo lost her footing. In his attempt to prevent her fall, Prince Cuilin inadvertently caught her sleeve, leading to the tear in her ru. This act, born of concern and quick reflexes, was unfortunately misinterpreted by Magistrate Lei upon his arrival. There was no crime; the prince's actions were misconstrued in a moment of urgency and confusion."

"Is this the truth of what happened, Prince?" Lord Yan asked, his voice breaking the hush that had fallen over the room. Cuilin met Lord Yan's gaze with a composure fitting of a prince of Zhou.

His voice was steady as he spoke, "I am aware that my actions breached social and customary boundaries, Lord Yan. However, my only intention was to safeguard your daughter from harm's way and shield her from the storm. Nothing more," he explained.

Lord Yan turned to Yinuo, "Is what he states true, daughter," he stressed.

Acknowledging their moment of intimacy would only bring disgrace and shame to them both, a thought that turned her stomach. If she revealed the kiss, then even Danbei's testimony that protected both her and Cuilin's reputation would be shattered. Yinuo cast her eyes down. Fine. At most, she'd lose him forever. She'd lost him once; what was another time? Her eyes reached for Prince Cuilin, and she saw him hesitate with a tip of a word on his lips, barely audible and more of a breath than a syllable.

"It's as Danbei says," she uttered. "Thank you, Danbei, for bringing this to light."

"See, Father, let us return to the wedding banquet and forget this unpleasant conversation," Danbei beamed. He bowed to Magistrate Lei, "Brother-in-law, thank you for defending my sister's honor. I am glad to have found such an upstanding friend."

"I am glad to have a brother-in-law who is committed to revealing the truth as well and for understanding the gravity of this manner," he returned the bow.

A small cough, interrupted the pleasantries. Yinuo felt it too, resonating in the words the cat-like purer said. "This matter is not easily settled," Lord Nie stated.

"Lord Nie, the matter is settled. Come enjoy the feast with us again," Danbei suggested, aiming to brush aside the man's concerns before he could change the topic.

"It is my son who has been insulted," he stated. "The prince's reputation and honor has been marred by this situation. Would it not be forthcoming to offer consolation for this matter?"

Lord Yan weighed it. "Of course, as it should be. What do you suggest to make amends for this shame?"

Lord Nie cleared his throat, "We find ourselves marred by misunderstandings and false accusations. The truth of the matter lies in Prince Cuilin's unimpeachable character; he is an exemplar of duty and integrity. Had it not been for his timely intervention, we might have faced a regrettable incident on this day of significance," he began, his gaze sweeping over the court members present to this statement. The whole world would know the request by the end of the day, and it made Yinuo's breath hitch as she focused on the small man.

"While Young Master Danbei's testimony has been invaluable in clarifying the nature of the events, it's crucial to acknowledge that he wasn't the only observer. Others, such as Magistrate Lei, have already demonstrated a propensity to misconstrue Prince Cuilin's and Miss Yan's interactions, casting shadows where none should exist. Given the influence and reach of such individuals, the potential for rumors to proliferate and tarnish the reputations of both Prince Cuilin and Miss Yan cannot be underestimated. Their characters and future prospects stand at the precipice, vulnerable to the court of public opinion, which, as we all know, can be both capricious and merciless. To leave this matter unresolved would not only harm their reputations but also cast a lingering shadow of impropriety over them."

Lord Nie then shifted slightly, his voice softening but retaining its persuasive edge. "In the spirit of good faith and to quell the tongues of rumor, please reconsider our proposal. Such a marriage would not only dispel any doubts of their conduct but also stand as a testament to our families' unity and mutual respect. It is, after all, a matter of protecting Miss Yan's reputation as much as it is about restoring Prince Cuilin's honor."

Yinuo could hear her heart in her ears. Her father's breath hitched in his throat, and he chuckled at the response. "This is convenient, isn't it? For Prince Cuilin to use the unfortunate circumstances to coerce our family into a marriage agreement! And what of the rumors that you've been conducting a scheme to please the Emperor!"

"If it were a scheme, why would your own son be the one to exonerate mine?" Lord Nie said, lifting his eyes to him. The room tensed, awaiting the fallout from such a blunt accusation.

Lei Yingzhe, spoke up, "Master Yan, if I may give insight as a Minister of Justice? Young Master Danbei acted in the interest of justice and truth without any thought of manipulating the situation toward this outcome. What benefit does he have for coming forward in defense of

Prince Cuilin, if not only to protect his sister? Can your family not consider that this proposal, rather than being a ploy, is actually a gesture towards resolving the situation with dignity and honor for all involved?"

Lord Yan raked his hands through his hair, "I gave you my answer. I will not entertain proposals until after this day has passed...However, Magistrate Lei, I hear your wisdom. I may have been rash, Prince Cuilin. I apologize. You are a guest, and your character did not need to be criticized." He softened and sighed. He turned to them, and Yinuo could almost think the matter settled, "Danbei, take your sister from this room. We shall revisit this conversation at a later time, under less... charged circumstances."

"Yes, father," he replied. He gestured for her to follow. Yinuo did, carefully walking out of the heavy air, but not removing herself completely. She stood at the door, and then shared a look with her brother.

"Danbei...why did you—"she started, but he covered her mouth. For an intense moment, her brother stared into her eyes carefully, judging for himself before finally speaking with her.

"You're reckless," he stated.

"I...I know, but I had to know, brother. I—"

"He is not Dehai," Danbei stressed. "I have to return to the other guests. Go to your room and wait for me there. I'll talk to you tomorrow. Please, sister, trust me."

"You saw us..." Yinuo awed, "Brother, why didn't you say anything?"

"Because I understand," he stated firmly, his voice trailing off as he departed. Yinuo lingered for a heartbeat, her gaze fixed on the hall through which he disappeared. Then, with a sudden resolve, she diverted her path, her steps quick and quiet as she navigated through an adjoining room, moving towards the unsettling silence that blanketed the side quarters.

Reaching the threshold of her father's study, she cautiously slid open a panel of the wooden screen just enough to allow her a glimpse inside. Her father struck Cuilin with such force that he crumpled to the floor. No one moved to intervene, not even his father. Lord Yan stood over him, imposing and cold.

"You are nothing," Lord Yan declared, his voice cutting through the tension, relentless and devoid of warmth. "Nothing but a hostage who breathes solely by the Emperor's grace! Your defiance has not gone unnoticed. Unless you yearn for death, Prince of Zhou, curb these selfish acts at once."

Yinuo's hand flew to her mouth, stifling the gasp that fought to escape as a mix of horror and disbelief washed over her. She observed as Cuilin struggled to his elbow, his gaze fierce, yet overshadowed by the shades who judged him. "I have only acted upon the Emperor's orders," he countered, his voice laden with resilience.

"See the Prince to his quarters," Lord Yan commanded dismissively. The guards, in a swooping motion, descended upon Cuilin, dragging him away with chilling indifference.

Yinuo retreated from the room, pushing off and running towards the back of the house. She slipped her way through the servants' quarters, where the raucous conversations of the Main Hall distilled into mere gleeful murmurs as she navigated through the dimming light of the setting sun towards where the prince was housed.

As she reached the prince's assigned room, a muffled scream pierced the stillness, followed by the unmistakable sound of something heavy collapsing against the floor. Heart in her throat, Yinuo pressed against the door, only to meet resistance. With determined effort, she forced apart the sliding door, which finally gave way to reveal the dimly lit room. There, in the sparse light filtering through the window, she found him at the desk, a mere shadow with his head cradled in his palm. Heavy chains encircled his wrists, glinting in the dim light.

Chains

11

Yinuo's heart skipped a beat. From her vantage point at the top of the steps, peering down into the sparsely decorated room, she saw him gently placing his hands on a low desk. The red marks around his wrist from where the metal encased them gripped her heart. Yet, he hadn't noticed her. A noise caught her attention, and she instinctively squatted against the wall to hide her shadow. Gently, she pacified her fear by tapping her racing heart and then turned to see the prince alone in the solitary room.

"Yinuo," Prince Cuilin breathed, and she picked herself up, dousing the lamp and sealing the door behind her. She rushed in but stopped before she passed the window, dropping to her knees.

"What are you doing?"

She tapped her finger to her lip and pointed at a house servant who walked past as Yinuo crawled her way to the side, out of view. When she reached her destination, she sat up and peered again out into the courtyard. The sunken room had walls that came just over her shoulders. No better than a dog pen, she thought. She shut the blinds and stepped back to face the prince, once again taking in his form. Thankfully, she observed no bruising visible through his clothes, and the marks around his hands were mere chafing rather than cuts.

"Let me find the key, they can't have hidden it far," Yinuo said, quietly. She started with the bookcases around the desk, and searching some of the potted plants.

The prince silently observed her, waiting in a stationary position to not raise the alarm. He kept his focus on Yinuo, and his lips sealed. Yinuo moved past him and got to her tiptoes to find the key hanging behind the decorative screen behind the prince. Dust lay in the crevices of the panel, but the main purpose of it was to hide the other instruments behind it.

Yinuo jumped back as Cuilin caught her arm. "Are you all right? What...what are you doing here?"

"I'm fine. I came because I saw what my father did. I couldn't let them hurt you. So here, we have to get you out of here. They didn't use any of those on you, did they?"

"No," he replied, still in awe of her.

Yinuo slipped the key into position and slide the lock from his arms, discarding it with a kick of her small foot into a dusty corner. Prince Cuilin flicked his hands a few times and rubbed his wrist, but otherwise took a seat back down at the desk.

"Thank you," he said in disbelief.

"You need to run," Yinuo implored him.

He hesitated, "Miss Yan..."

"Stop it. I will not allow you to suffer because of my impulsiveness!"

"I kissed you," he replied.

"I initiated!"

"I reciprocated!" he interjected in a raised voice that silenced her. Her shoulders fell forward as she knelt next to him. Yinuo couldn't leave him like this, but she didn't know what to do. Softly, Cuilin opened his mouth again, the words like a cruel cut, "A gentleman would have pushed you back. I—"

"Don't you dare apologize!" she retorted, "I don't regret it. So please, don't make me feel like I've done you a great disservice. Don't make me feel like...like an idiot who kissed a stranger."

"That was never my intent," he softly replied.

"I won't have you mistreated. I know that they'll look for any excuse to punish you, even if they've dropped the charges. So run, I'll help you run. I know you suffer from fatigue but lean on me. I can get you out of here."

He presented his palms to her, "You may have freed me, but my wrists are still bound. Leaving won't change that."

Yinuo's eyes widened. "There are knives," she whispered, "and other tools behind that screen. Who's to say they won't change their minds!"

"The misunderstanding has already been cleared," he replied, curling his hands into a fist. "The Emperor will learn of what happened today, and I may be on his bad side, but he knows what he leverages with hosting me. I am both hostage and charge."

Yinuo looked around the pen, the shoddy excuse of a spare room. What person deserved this kind of treatment? She clasped her hand to her forehead. "Because of my rashness, I lost a dear friend...I..." For a moment, she stopped herself, too embarrassed to explain clearly what she wanted or intended. She didn't want him to be hurt because of her. She never wanted there to be a misunderstanding, but...she didn't regret the kiss. "Let me help you escape," she whispered her plea.

"My position shields me," he began in a low tone, "I appreciate the concern, but I have endured worse."

"What else could you have endured?" she asked.

He thought for a minute, "My family willingly agreed for me to being taken hostage. I am not the heir nor even the first choice. I am merely a son of Zhou who is expendable. While the Emperor believes me a valuable asset my country plants hexes in my room to assassinate me and declare the treaty void. I was chosen as a scapegoat for my country, a delicate political play in a shaky alliance."

"Your family wants to sacrifice you?" she awed, reliving her careless words of being apart from everyone who has ever loved you. She bowed her head in shame, truly she knew nothing of his suffering.

"If I am in the Emperor's favor, I will live to be a toothless man. If I lose favor, then I will leave a beautiful corpse. I have lived with the court for several years, I have a better understanding of the Emperor's temperament, and besides, this was worth it to see you again."

Could hope bite her heart and make her want to see what she wanted in the face of a man whose scars lured her closer to him? Being so close, his scent, a mix of peony and musk, beat her heart in remembering how soft his lips had been upon her. How "right" it had all felt a moment ago despite the fear of losing him again. "What do you mean?" she asked.

He went quiet, curling his fingers into a fist on the desk. "When I first saw you, I saw a woman smiling so brightly to a peony. Your face was buried in the petals, and I thought how free you were even though I was a little drowsy from medicine," he explained. Yet, the hesitation in his voice made her curious, what was he holding back?

"...Are you Dehai?" she asked, the words falling out of her mouth before she could stop herself. She held his stare, reaching for his hand, but he recoiled it from her.

"You should leave, Yinuo. Before someone misunderstands."

"Then tell me, what are you holding back?"

"I knew I liked you from the moment I saw you, but I do not think that my situation is worthy of such a free-spirited heart. One who loves peonies and her brothers so fiercely that she would become a hostage with me. What right do I have to have any spark of feelings for someone so free?"

"Then why did you propose to my father if all of these things hold you back?" she asked.

"Because I am a fool. Lord Nie has been ordered by the Emperor to find me a suitable bride. I am merely following the Emperor's orders. However, Lord Nie is my uncle. He asked me my opinion, and I am sorry. I shouldn't have—I am merely a prince who, on his first birthday, chose a peony instead of the seal."

"How does choosing a peony condemn you?" she raised her voice. "How is appreciating beauty and nature so horrible of a choice! I'd stay with anyone who chose a peony for a thousand lifetimes compared to one who chose a brush, arrow, or seal. At least then, I'd know he'd know what is good and worthwhile in the world. What is wrong with a peony? You tell me you admire my free spirit. What if I look at you and want to free you, too!"

"Please, don't raise your voice, I don't—" he held up his arms.

"Ask me what I want," she ordered him.

"W-What do you want?"

"I want to be with my king of flowers again," she said, tears falling from her face. Wrapping her arms around his neck and pulling him to her, she brought his lips to hers. His arms touched her back—an invasion of space not unwelcome. When she dipped her head, breaking the kiss, she continued, "My freedom is an illusion; I live trapped in my role as a daughter in a noble house. But if I could share it, then I do not think this weight would be a burden, but merely a memory of the past."

The back of his palm reached for her neck, cupping the sensitive skin at the base of her ear. While intense eyes never left her face or the flush forming at her cheeks. She did not hear him confirm; instead, she felt a return of pressure, softness at her cheeks, and sweetness on her lips. The world was right again, the light rain in the distance, rapping on the roof; she lost herself in her senses, returning her passion to her king of flowers again.

Absolution
12

For a moment, in the warm rays of sunlight casting light and shadows over Prince Cuilin's scars, Yinuo felt at peace. She'd reclaimed a piece of her heart, even with the ache at her core. As fleeting as the discomfort, morning returned, and she knew what she risked as she brushed a lock from his face and gently kissed him again. Drawing herself away, she felt a grip on her wrist and looked to see the prince's hand clutching hers.

He didn't say anything, his eyes studying her own, a look filled with both desperation and longing. Of words at the tip of his tongue, but still he refrained. Yinuo brushed his cheek and then planted another kiss where she had gently stroked him.

"I have to go," she whispered. She stood, but the grip did not leave her wrist. Inhaling slowly, she allowed the moment to be, just for a moment, just for all the moments that she'd given up when she had lost him.

And though part of her felt loss, the other felt a tug as he laid her across his chest. He ran his fingers through her hair and pressed his forehead to hers. "Stay," he cooed.

Sliding her head against his, she felt the salt on his skin tugging a little at hers. Almost as if a manifestation that gently resisted the separation. She couldn't stay. Yinuo pushed herself up and firmly gripped his hands before making her way to the stairs. She opened the door and peeked her head out to the hallway. Then, stepping out without bothering to shut it behind her or greet the servants whom she approached from behind, she moved silently. At the first window, she slipped through the screen and made her way back to her own room.

Her only focus was getting to her room without being discovered and changing into plain clothes—a sudden urgency gripped her heart, driving her to confirm the source of her unease. She'd spent the night with Prince Cuilin, embraced in passions that blushed her cheeks. But no, the act, for all its pleasures, failed to dispel her doubts. Yinuo quickly discarded her clothes and washed her body with the water at the basin before getting dressed to investigate her qualm.

The house slept, all except her and possibly Mingdan, but she had to confront the disquiet, so once again, she slipped out of her window and passed her brother's room. At the wall, the General's Báijiǔ barrels were still stacked high enough for her to escape—the same ones she had used the first time she left. Yinuo silently lifted herself onto the first when, from behind, her arm was grasped.

"Where have you been?" Mingdan's voice rang clear.

"Let me go," she said, unable to face him.

"Father has half the guests looking for you!"

"Let me go, Mingdan!" she demanded, ripping her arm from his grasp. Without looking back, Yinuo lunged to the next barrel, pulling herself onto the roof with Mingdan trailing close behind. A roof tile escaped its place as she rolled off the wall, punctuated by a loud crack as it broke.

"Wait!" Mingdan urged. He chased after her, quickly catching up to grasp her shoulders, but she sidestepped him. Rushing as fast as her legs could carry her, she didn't care that he followed even when his breaths grew labored. At a crossroads, she stopped to reorient herself.

"Huff...huh, so where are we going?" he asked between breaths and clutching his chest.

Yinuo turned on him. "I have to confirm something."

"Okay," he replied. Yinuo's expression softened. "I will accompany you. It is a beautiful morning for a walk—"Yinuo darted off. "Or run! We'll run; just wait for me!"

Yinuo led her brother outside of the town, where the green fields were sprouting their first crops over the rolling hills. Without prompting, Mingdan asked a local farmer, who'd bought supplies from town, to allow them to ride on his cart to the village. The world was dampened with mist, creating a cool that drifted over them, manifesting into a silence as they sat at the back of the cart. Yinuo gripped her hands together, and slowly, he placed his own on top of hers in silent camaraderie.

She focused on the road, butterflies in her stomach, as her brother's concern turned to watch what lay ahead. The cart pulled up to the edge of the village as the last of sunrise's hues cleared to an endless blue sky. Yinuo hopped off before the cart came to a stop, and Mingdan followed, catching her arm to right her balance. The ochre wall of the village stood watch while Mingdan studied it, and Yinuo marched along a side path. Their uphill challenge, overgrown with weeds and laid with dirt, followed the wall's outskirts.

Breaking through the overgrowth, the siblings came to an old, neglected home. The once proud gate was absent from its post, and the remains were splintered on the side. Yinuo stepped through the threshold, focusing on the whistling wind through the fluttering panels with their paper flaking from their rectangular grids. The walls were marred with cracks and crevices of a shifting foundation and mold that penetrated the home.

Looking on, the black mouth opened where an interior door should have greeted them. The only sentinels that guarded the pavilion were patches of purslane, their fleshy leaves and reddish stems spreading among the gravel, displaying tiny yellow flowers that were overcoming the once well-maintained stone.

Yinuo took a step forward when her brother caught her arm. "You don't have to do this," he said. She shook him off and then knelt in front of the home with clasped hands. "Dehai. I'm sorry."

Knees in the mud, Yinuo begged for absolution. The house, believed to be cursed, once homed the gardener and his son, as evidenced by the unruly peonies that sprawled from their original beds. Their crimes invoked a cruel order, extending their torture to having their remains laid out in the open and their spirits to wander as èguĭ.

From where Mingdan stood, he saw a board and a rectangle that he wouldn't have even noticed if it weren't for his sister. It took him a moment to understand; these were makeshift graves, a silent protest against the Emperor's cruel decree. Yinuo had constructed them to honor the gardener and his son with this simple memorial, preventing their spirits from wandering. Occupied with these revelations, he didn't have time to react when Yinuo slammed her head into the ground and lifted it with tears in her eyes.

Mingdan rushed to her side, taking her shoulders and carefully embracing her. He pulled her chin up and saw the patches of mud on her face and redness from striking a stone. Cautiously, he took the hem of his sleeve and wiped it away. Then he brought her close, stroking the back of her hair—but otherwise, standing in silent solidarity.

He never knew, no one knew, she'd done this for them. A deep sense of regret and guilt washed over Mingdan for not being there for his sister. "Tell me what happened."

Yinuo shook her head. "I'm an idiot. I tried to get back something that had been taken from me by replacing it. He's not Dehai. He'll never be him. Why? Why am I tortured like this? Why did I like it? Why did it feel right!" she shouted, breaking down in her brother's arms. "Dehai is dead! Dehai is dead! Dehai is dead!" she called her hollow refrain, clutching him. "I cannot have him back! I cannot make up for what they did to him! I cannot have him! I don't deserve it! I don't!"

Mingdan let the tears run their course. "Yinuo," her brother said softly.

"He's dead..." she uttered, her voice a bare whisper above the songbirds around her. Gently, she broke the contact with her brother, rubbing the side of her face and looking at the garden that had been neglected, but also filled with peonies so bright and vibrant. It almost felt like they were trying to comfort her. How could the world be so beautiful and disgusting at the same time? That's what she felt. Disgusted.

For years and years, she had been susceptible during the season of peonies to these episodes of melancholy. However, they appeared as a passing thought in her head. One that could be pushed out and ignored, like an annoyance in the wind.

Prince Cuilin had changed that.

His presence had constantly reminded her of her wish—that Dehai was alive, but she knew the truth. She always knew it, and still...

Her brother put some distance between them, wiping down her face and tilting her chin to look at him again. "Yinuo? What do you need from me?"

"How can my wish be answered?" she asked, an overwhelming sense of hopelessness embedding itself in her heart. "How can I be with my king of flowers again?"

"I'm afraid I do not have those answers, but whatever happens, we're here, Yinuo. We'll get you through this."

"I'm so reckless."

"En, that is my jiějiě," he replied. With one last surge of pressure, he released her from his grasp. He stood before the graves, "I am taking my sister home now. Please return to peace, and know no matter what she does. She is always my sister. So please continue to watch over her."

Mingdan took her hand and slowly walked towards the gate, where Yinuo paused. Looking back, a shaft of light illuminated a peony in the breeze. She swore she saw a glimmer, but Mingdan's gentle tug pulled her from her thoughts. "It'll be late when we get home. Perhaps we can stay in the village tonight."

Yinuo shook her head, "Let's go home."

"Is your leg going to make the journey?" he asked.

"I've endured worse," she replied softly. "But thank you for your concern. Mingdan, will you tell father about this?"

"No," he replied. "Father doesn't deserve it after making his only daughter cry."

"And Prince Cuilin? What do I do about it?" she asked.

"My sister doesn't open her heart to anyone, but when she does, she does so fully without thinking of the next moment. You live reckless, but you live true to your desires. I know you will do what your heart calls despite what other's will desire. And I stand by my word; whatever comes, we'll stand with you, Yinuo."

Before she could respond, a distant yelling came from the ridge line. They looked up to the call and saw Weixin riding their father's black steed at full pace. He wore his armor and, more shocking, had his sword at his side. "What is Weixin doing there?" she asked.

"Gēgē!" Mingdan flagged him down. The horse passed them in the gutter as Mingdan deftly maneuvered them out of the stamping steed. Weixin flung himself from his horse, letting it trot off, and threw his arms around Yinuo.

"Yinuo!" he cried. "Oh, thank heavens!"

"What? What is it, brother?"

"Are you unharmed? Why are you covered in mud?" he asked. "Never mind that! Mingdan! We have to return to father!"

"What is the matter?" Mingdan asked.

"Prince Cuilin has been accused of abducting Yinuo! He is going to be punished! We have to save him! Come!" he grabbed Yinuo's arm and headed for the horse when she tore her arm from him.

"Why is he accused of that!" she demanded.

"Yinuo, we don't have time!"

"Why is he accused of abducting me! How would he have the resources to do so! He's just a prisoner of the Emperor and Father and everyone!"

"That's why we must hurry! They found your ru and blood in his room this morning! The minister of justice has arrested him and is going to torture him to find your location! Please, Yinuo!" He begged; then suddenly his face fell. "You weren't harmed by him, were you?"

Yinuo fervently shook her head. "No, I was not harmed by him. Now! Take me to him! We have to stop this!" she cried.

"Mingdan! Ask the village leader to lend you a horse with your seal! He'll understand! I have to take Yinuo now!"

"Understood, go!" Mingdan called, rushing back towards the village. Weixin swept Yinuo into his arms and sat her in front of him. He pushed the horse hard, the labored breathing and racing heart against her thighs.

"Weixin!" she called, fearful of the hills and the force that made her feel as if she would be dislodged at any moment. She sat in front of her brother with nothing to grasp onto, spare for the horn.

"It's okay!" Weixin reassured her. "We're going to make it!"

"Weixin, why are you doing this for the prince?" she asked.

"He saved my life, mèimei. When he was forced to join the front lines to defend both his country and ours, his brother ambushed and tried to capture him. I was with the battalion, among the men who had been taken with the Prince. He pleaded for my life when he could have easily let me be killed. His brother slaughtered my men in cold blood, but Prince Cuilin stood in front of the blade for me! That's the reason for the scar across his face," Weixin quickly explained. "It gave me enough time to free myself from my bindings and get him to safety. I won't let him die now!" he shouted.

"He...he saved you," she mused.

"Hold tight!" Weixin shouted. Yinuo gripped the horse as it leaped past a fence and sent it flying downhill. Her stomach lifted into her chest and forced the air from her lungs. She gripped the horn, closing her eyes, which made it worse, but they tore through the field and the gate that had swung open. They raced past their home, Weixin struggling with something on his belt.

"Where are we going?! The house is the other way!"

"We're not going to the house," Weixin called, his whistle cutting sharply through the air. Answering his summons, his men appeared beside them with raised spears as they charged toward a massive red gate. Yinuo's heart lurched— she recognized the grandeur of the palace's red walls.

Unyielding, her brother flashed his seal at the guards posted without so much as pause while his men barreled through them after. Led by a black stallion, fifty soldiers created a thunderous stampede through the palace's gilded courtyard in a torrent of clattering hooves that announced their arrival.

In the direct path of their charge, her hair tousled by the force, Yinuo lifted her gaze to the immense palace reigning atop a colossal hill. Its imposing statue was further accentuated by the pristine, tiered steps leading towards it. The horse took the steps effortlessly, its heartbeat pulsing against her legs as her brother's grip intensified at her waist.

The eunuchs at the door exchanged a brief, stoic look before pulling the main gate wide open, allowing the mud-splattered horse entry into the Great Hall. Yinuo's breath hitched; the Emperor's court was in full session, their proceedings shattered by their sudden intrusion. Murmurs escalated to cries as the horse reared, and Weixin expertly brought it under control.

But Yinuo could not take her eyes off the Emperor's commanding presence, who sat upon a massive gleaming throne. His presence stood as the eye of the storm, adorned in golden, layered dragon robes. Weixin tore her from the saddle and marched her down the aisle towards the Emperor, past her father's dismayed expression and the other court members, who were arrayed in rows according to their status and colored robes.

Around her, brows furrowed, and whispers of disgrace swirled through the hall, but Yinuo's eyes met the Emperor's own rich brown ones. She held his focus, a look of curiosity more than anger.

Embraced

13

Dehai is dead. How many times must that refrain continue, and the wish be taken away when it felt so close to her? Yinuo held her breath, restraining herself from lashing out at the man responsible for the order—the one who followed the law. His rich brown eyes commanded the world before him, including her. She'd place all the blame on him, if she could, but she had been the one to break the boundaries, no matter how innocent.

Her brother's words did not enter her ears, though the firm press of his hands at her shoulder placed both of them to kneel before the Emperor. She saw the carpet and the hem of his golden robes as her brother presented her as his sister. Yinuo raised her eyes to the man her neck caught by Weixin's palm, caught but not trapped. She lifted herself up as her brother remained kneeling. With a quick bow, she addressed the Emperor. "I am Yan Yinuo, the Eldest Daughter of Chancellor Yan. Forgive my lax in etiquette and excuse me from the protocols, for I do so out of desperation."

The Emperor did not rebuke her, and her father's tongue was held by the Emperor's gaze upon his daughter.

Yinuo breathed in, and said, "I have not been harmed by Zhou Prince. I went with my younger brother, Yan Mingdan, to pay respects at a family's grave early this morning, which is why I disappeared. I can explain everything. If you just grant a reprieve of the Zhou Prince's interrogation."

The Emperor studied her a moment, "Chancellor Yan, it relieves me greatly to see your daughter unscathed. I will permit your daughter to stand in court; however, that magnificent beast needs to find a home in the stables. Tell me, Yan Weixin, how old is the horse?"

"Your Grace—" Yinuo tried to speak up, when her brother caught her arm.

"The horse shares its age with my sister. Should it find favor in your eyes, I would be honored to gift it to you." Weixin explained. Yinuo gave her brother a look of disgust.

"Hrm, a foal derived from such a steed would suffice. It is apparent, Chancellor Yan, that your daughter does not know the entirety of the situation. However, let us not burden her. Yan Weixin, escort that beast out of my hall, and you," he turned to Yinuo as Weixin promptly obeyed the Emperor's command. "Come."

Yinuo followed, as the courtiers dispersed to their respective duties, with her father joining her side without so much of a word, but a furrowed expression. They marched together behind the Emperor and in front of his horde of servants. The Emperor turned to them, "We will proceed to the Hall of Justice, where Chancellor Yan's daughter shall present her account to Magistrate Lei. Regarding Zhou Prince's condition, I make no assurances." he said, then paused locking eyes with her, "Do not faint on me," he threatened. Yinuo nodded, feeling every syllable as a scorching cut; she clutched her heart to refrain from speaking out.

As the Emperor retreated into his palanquin, another arrived for Yinuo and her father. Her father slid across the seat, allowing her to step up next to him. When she was settled, he grasped her knee. Lord Yan looked to be on the verge of saying something, but instead he withheld it from her and turned to look away.

"Father—"

"Do not speak to me," he snapped.

"Why did you do this? Why did you assume that the prince had stolen me away!" she demanded.

"Sh!" he covered her mouth, but she tore her head from his hand, biting him to finally free herself.

"I know that Prince Cuilin needs a marriage for the alliance and his safety! I know that his family has sent assassins to break the treaty and that your own son was saved by him! We owe him. What are you hiding!"

Her father sighed, propping his elbow on the window sill and leaning his head into his palm. "We owe him nothing. He is merely a scavenger, barely clinging to the fringes of the Emperor's grace. We will not be affiliated with such a character."

"Is he Dehai?" she asked, unable to help herself.

"What are you talking about?"

"The gardener's son! He looks just like him! Is Prince Cuilin Dehai!"

"Have you gone mad?" he demanded. "I do not know a Dehai! We do not have time for this—!"

"The servant you killed! You had him flogged and then beheaded because I kissed him! Tell me! Is that the truth!

Why does he look like Prince Cuilin! Why does he pull at my heart!"

"Be quiet! There are others around, and they hear you!" he retorted.

"I will not! Not until you tell me the truth! Why did you send Prince Cuilin away! Was it because for the first time in a long time I actually felt my heart beat!" she shouted. She pounded on her father's chest. "Dammit, stop keeping things from me..."

Her father's lips quivered, but did not move. He shoved her from him, and turned again towards the window with his brows almost to the point of touching each other.

"Disown me," Yinuo whispered, "Next time I find someone in my heart, disown me. I'd prefer it."

The carriage came to a stop, and Yinuo bolted from it, falling out, but was caught by a servant stationed nearby. Yinuo didn't wait for anyone; instead, she ran towards the gate and into the courtyard of the Hall of Justice. The men at the door held up spears to her, and she hesitated. "I have permission to see Magistrate Lei!" she screeched.

The guards shared a look and then got to their knees. Yinuo didn't need to look behind her to know that the Emperor was approaching. Heavy footsteps filled the silent air; she didn't wait for him, sidestepping the guards and rushing into the hall. She passed offices and open spaces that she did not dare to register.

Driven only by the desire to see Cuilin and ensure that he wasn't hurt, she didn't know what she would do. But as she passed, each guard she met fell to their knees, the Emperor's approach growing more and more ominous. She felt like she was running from his shadow in a race against time, not knowing if she'd truly make it before the darkness devoured her.

A loud cry echoed through her, barely muffled by a door. There! She rushed towards the sound until the hall, through an archway, opened into a yard reeking of stale iron. Yinuo's knees locked, forcing her to view the scene before her. Prince Cuilin's face was bruised, with a split lip that dribbled down his chin and onto his white robes. Stripped of the fine silks, he wore a prisoner's tunic and pants, both disarrayed and stained with splatters of blood.

Around him, gravel had been cleared and piled up to form a pronounced border, creating an oval-shaped clearing. A layer of hay covered the exposed ground around and beneath the chair where Prince Cuilin was bound with rods securing his thighs. Shallow breaths escaped his lips as Prince Cuilin's head hung at his breast. Completely isolated—only the sound of his breathing disturbed the silence. A slight whistling encapsulated the space between him and Yinuo.

"Dehai!" she called to him, rushing to kneel before him, but not to weep, but to assess how to release the mechanism. She didn't focus on the stains on his body or look for anything else, hauling the rods out and searching for a way to take off the bindings. A flash of memory had her reaching for the knife he'd hidden in his belt, and she pricked herself before finding it within the folds. Gingerly, she removed it, keeping the blade's edge away from him. Once free, she sliced through the bindings around his wrists.

"This is not what I granted," the Emperor's cold voice said.

Yinuo pivoted, the blade still in her hand, her voice trembling with revulsion, "Is this the path to truth you've chosen? Where is the honesty in pain—it's disgusting and senseless!"

"I never promised anything about his condition," the Emperor replied. He folded his arm, but kept his distance from her. He blocked the hallway and the guards behind him. "Put down the knife."

"Is that all you can say!" she demanded. "Your treaty demands that the prince live! If he dies because of these injuries you will set upon your people turmoil and send Weixin to war!" she proclaimed.

"Miss Yan, I will forgive this heinous offense, but you must heed me. Drop the knife," the Emperor said, taking a single step forward.

Yinuo tightened, still gripping the small knife and holding her other arm back to defend him. "Stay back! I won't let you harm him—!"

A sharp, piercing pain exploded across her collarbone as an arrow struck, the force knocking her to the ground. "Assassin! Protect the Emperor!" Unable to respond, she looked up in time to see a man on the roof drawing his bow at Cuilin.

Without thinking, and all in an elongated moment, she threw herself towards Cuilin, focusing all her energies on seeing both Dehai and Cuilin as one. Their scars lining up, the smile of her beloved childhood friend, and the gentleness of peonies dampened her surroundings. She cradled him just in time as another arrow lodged itself into her back, sending a deep, throbbing pain across her chest, jerking her arms tight. Gasping for air—she hesitated to cast her eyes down; the arrow hadn't gone through.

"Yinuo!" Weixin cried—or was it Danbei's? But the agony flared, scorching through her. She could only draw her trembling hand to the unconscious face of Cuilin, brushing the silken lock from his face. His eyes opened for the first time to reveal sky-blue. The same blue that would have taken her to the Eastern Sea.

Cuilin blinked, coming into focus. "You bastard!" Weixin shouted. He stood on the rooftop, chasing down a man dressed in black garb.

Yinuo's breath caught. "Are...you..."

Cuilin grasped her face. "Yinuo!"

"Stay, Dehai...I want to stay..." she called, her eyes losing focus, and a light-headedness filling her. Her whole body quaked with pain. She lowered her head to see her strength falter. In that moment, as she leaned into Cuilin, her clothing tugged up, causing the front arrow to shift and dislodge itself. Her eyes closed, embraced by the rise of his chest, and enveloped in the musk of peonies.

"Yinuo!" he shouted, threading his fingers through her hair, "No, no!" He looked up to the soldiers who'd rushed the courtyard, among them, her father and brother Danbei, but they kept their distance. Cuilin stood, embracing Yinuo to his body. "What are you doing standing there! Move!" he demanded. The guards lowered their spears at him, taking a slow ascent towards them.

"Give me back my daughter!" Lord Yan shrieked from behind the line, his face a swollen red, almost to the shade of purple.

Cuilin's grip tightened. "Never," he retorted, "I will never give Yi'er back!" His shout rose a gust of wind staggering the guards. As instantly, from the ground crimson stalks rapidly sprung from the hay and dirt, sending gravel flying in its haste. The tiny projectiles peppering those impeding the circle. The stalks with their crimson tapered ends like spines, pierced through the air, rapidly developing into full brush blocking the path of the soldiers to Cuilin. Just as suddenly, darkness covered the sun, centering over the palace and all that lay within.

Cuilin's eyes firmed, and he tightened his grip on Yinuo's waist in both protective and possessiveness. A torrent whipped clothes and flared hair, creating a vent that pushed all who tried to approach. He turned to Yinuo to brush her face as the men's screams became a void in a red gale around them.

Cuilin pressed his forehead to hers. "I want to stay too," he cried, tears dewing from his eyes. "I want to stay, but I can't, Yinuo..."

The flesh of his arm holding Yinuo began to dissolve into gentle red swirls, no longer able to sustain its grip on her. Franticly, his other arm shot out, reaching her just in time to gradually take her down so she lay in his arms. With one quick motion, he yanked the remaining arrow from her back. Desperately, he pressed his face to hers. "Yinuo..."

She saw him disappearing, the energies and the lights replacing the contours of his body. Gently, she reached for his face, traced the scars at his forehead, and then trailed down to his chin. She felt herself flatten to the ground without his support, but his torso still held onto this world.

"I love you, Dehai. I will always love you," she replied, catching a lock of his hair. She drew herself up, and met his soft lips to hers, one last kiss. One last wish, to be with her king of flowers again.

Yinuo!" the voice called out. Darkness surrounded her, a numbness that she couldn't explain. But even in the void, she saw before her the back of her childhood form—the little girl with a broad smile who turned to her before rushing forward. She collided with the back of a little boy, hugging him deeply, her giggles filling the world. Slowly, the two children faded away, leaving only the man who watched on the other side.

"Dehai," she breathed, clutching her hand into a fist. Her eyes rose to where he stood, dressed so finely and just a few steps away. His bright blue eyes were a beacon against the void, threatening to overwhelm her. As he came into view, she sensed something different about him.

From Cuilin, an energy haloed his form, casting a subtle glow. He wore a red vest layered over blue, accentuating the color of his eyes. Beneath those robes, a collection of gauze-like, fine sheer silks fluttered in the invisible wind. Every inch of the silks were embroidered with the most delicate golden peonies—some mere outlines, while others detailed into every intricate petal.

His hair, styled in a high ponytail and caught by an invisible wind, was secured with both a matching ribbon and an organic hairpin made from spring stalks. A large peony, placed at the side of his head, balanced his appearance, while his ears were adorned with strands of silver and crimson beads, ending in blue tassels.

He cast out his hand, and the head of a red peony with a golden center blossomed in the air above it. The flower was suspended over his palm, and petals fluttered around it, bursting into glittering lights, all encased by a symphony of red swirls.

She should have been fearful; she recognized the power he wielded, the elegance that announced his presence. Yet, the ache in her heart and the deep-set longing within her soul were stronger. For the briefest of moments, she worried he might disappear, that the heavens would once again be cruel to her.

But it was the thought of losing him that truly languished within her, overshadowing all else. She wanted to be with him—to hold him once more, to accept the peony as a token of his love, presented with such grace.

"Thank heavens, thank heavens you've said it," he spoke. Yinuo took her chance, reaching through the void, pulling and willing herself to live. She grasped his hand and breathed relief as his presence enveloped her; from the mild warmth to the sweet scent, it consumed her being and dulled the pain. They stilled.

Cuilin brought his warmth to her as he wrapped her in his arms, and then everything, everything radiated perfection. Right where she stood, no matter what happened, Yinuo knew what her heart desired, but she also had questions she had never been given answers to. "Where have you been?" she asked.

He brushed the tears from her face. "Trying to get back to you."

"I saw...I saw you die," she choked on her words. Gently, he stroked away another tear, still embracing her in warmth.

"I am whole," he replied. "I saw you dying...I thought that I would lose you again."

"You're not hurt?" she choked.

"I have obtained my true form, so no, I am no longer in pain," he explained. Yinuo brushed his arms and then took his face in her hands. She sought his eyes and traced the faint white lines that bared the scars of his life. Delicately, she placed her thumb to the one on his chin.

"Is it really you?" she uttered.

"En. It's me," he replied, cupping her hand and turning his head to kiss her palm. "I'm staying, Yinuo. I can finally stay."

"I don't understand, and I'm scared. What is all this? What has happened?"

He held her at length, searching her eyes and watching as the tears disappeared into the nothingness. "Don't be frightened. I'll explain everything to you. I can finally say it."

"Start with something recent. Tell me why you were beaten and bloodied in that yard," she said. He rubbed her shoulders, carefully forming his words, but not withholding them.

"Magistrate Lei betrayed me," he explained. "He's been conspiring with my earthly step-brother to break the treaty. Magistrate Lei left the interrogation so that a Zhou assassin could take my life and line his pockets. By doing so, he could earn favor with your father, ensuring his engagement to you, but you...you stood before the arrows meant for me. If not for you," he tucked her hair behind her ear, "That is not important now. I have no purpose in the world of men now that I have what I've always desired."

"And that is?"

With one hand, he carefully stripped the tears from her face. "Yinuo, do you know what I am?"

"You're a peony," she said.

"Close enough. I am a Peony Spirit," he replied. Her brows furrowed, and he continued, "I wasn't always a spirit; I can remember being the son of a gardener and his love and care for the plants he cultivated. I was innocent when they took that life."

Yinuo shuddered, pressing her head against his chest.

"It wasn't your fault," he whispered, "Can I explain?"

She slowly nodded.

"The peonies witnessed it. They saw the cruelty. They asked heaven for another chance for me. However, even though I would come into their clan, I could not part with my earthly desires to be loved by you. How would it have been fair to only have been a flower in your garden? I didn't want that. I rejected it. Though to be washed away to a new life, I was restless, and to save myself from lashing out at the living, I was offered a test.

"I was placed into Prince Cuilin's life for one purpose: to prove I could earn our love again. Do not fear. I've passed— we've passed," he stated.

"So, you're a form of Dehai and Cuilin together?" she mused. "A second chance, but a new person?"

"Who has always had you in his heart."

"Even as Cuilin?" she asked.

"En, call me what you wish. As long as you continue to call me, I will be content," he said.

"There's only one thing I don't understand. Why did you keep this from me?" she inquired, not meeting his eyes. She focused at his chest, carefully laying her hand there. She wanted to press her head against it and confirm that his heart beat in her ear.

"Fear," he confessed. "I didn't want to hurt you again. I understand what Dehai went through defies logic, and I couldn't bring myself to say it. I'm not Dehai," he stopped, pausing for her. "I'm something changed and new. I feared you would deny me, of course, but I feared more losing you entirely. Besides, you told me yourself your heart was as withered as a peony because of me. I cried over that," he drew her closer.

"No more," she wiped her face, then smoothed out his clothes, brushing his shoulders. "You always came back to me in the spring."

"Always," he said. Yinuo watched as Cuilin presented her with the peony again, but this time, a green glow folded it in on itself, and he curled his fingers around the small bead of light. When he opened his hands again, there lay a carved jade peony ring with a filigree golden band. Yinuo nodded, slipping it around her thumb, admiring the shine that fell over each and every carved petal. The sidebands revealed phoenixes' reliefs of gold and tiny specks of jade eyes.

She smiled, this time a joy filling her heart. Her tears were spent, and she shook her head, laying it once more against his heartbeat. "I feel tired."

He nodded, "You can rest."

"I don't feel any pain," she stated, lifting the arm that had been struck.

"This is only a transient reprieve. Will you come with me, please?" he asked softly.

"I've only ever had one wish, Dehai, and that was to be with my king of flowers again. Let us walk together," she replied. He kissed her forehead, drawing her eyelids closed. Opening her eyes to the light, Yinuo stood with the Peony Spirit Dehai, Cuilin, whole and adorned with the garments he'd had in the void.

Pressed against his chest, his arm around her waist, she felt his lips graze the tip of her cheek. The shadows encroaching her space were struggling against the large spires of peony stalks that had created a perimeter around them. They were back, she realized, unable to process everything completely. A numbness that imbued her, but a fear that forced her to grasp his robes tightly.

At that moment, the haze lifted from her senses; she realized who he was focusing on, not the Emperor or his guards, but her brothers—Danbei and Weixin. Weixin had a scrape on his cheek, his blade hacking through the massive peonies that hindered their advance. "Cuilin!" he shouted.

"Thank you, Weixin. You were a good friend," he replied. "I always knew you'd make a fine general one day."

Weixin's eyes widened in fear. "What do you mean! Cuilin!"

Danbei caught his shoulder and shook his head. "Let them go."

"She's hurt! Yi'er!" Weixin cried. He fought with the peonies, pushed into the weeds, but the stalks curled, and captured his heels. They wrapped around Weixin's calves and brought him down to his knees. A sudden heaviness forced Yinuo's eyes to shadow, and she saw the raw wounds at her chest. It's okay, Weixin ge, she wanted to reassure him. She'd made her choice. "Yi'er!" he thrashed out, calling in panic and pain.

"I'm taking my bride home," he replied calmly.

With that final note, the world shifted, red swirls devoured them, and Yinuo clung to Cuilin as he raised to torrent, casting the peonies around them and bursting them into a rain of petals. They disappeared into the mist, Weixin breaking free from the stalks just in time to reach where they had been.

The storm settled, covering the yard with a blanket of peony petals, even on Weixin's shoulder, as he stood beguiled by the image in front of him. The sun returned, casting a beam through the clouds and onto a single surviving blossom. A perfectly prepared token lay at the feet of the chair where his sister had been just a moment before.

A defiance, stark and beautiful—a peony.

About the Author

Anne Katih creates fantastical worlds that bridge her love for culture and drama. Inspired by her travels, as well as her passion for art and history, her writing is filled with rich, captivating narratives. When she's not immersed in her stories, Anne enjoys collecting sculptures, experimenting with various art forms, and exploring the depths of anthropology. Her unique perspective brings depth and authenticity to her work.

Connect with Anne Katih:
Instagram: @authorannekatih
Website: honeylocustbooks.com
Email: contact@honeylocustbooks.com

Also by Anne Katih

REED OF THE WILLOW 🌿

Dai Juna's world of secretive endeavors and mercantile
challenges is upended by a man with shattered memories
and a cascade of murder and intrigue.

WARD OF STORMS ☁

In a land of ancient cultivation and mystical beings, Xinrui
must prove her innocence with the help of a magnificent,
storm-controlling Qilin.

SIMPLE AS SNOW ❄

A fire caster's heart is ignited by a southern prince pursued
by a sorceress intent on devouring his heart's fire.

Discover more at honeylocustbooks.com

GENERAL TERMS

Báijiǔ (白酒): A traditional Chinese distilled alcoholic beverage, known for its strong flavor. It is commonly made from sorghum.

En (嗯): A versatile expression used to indicate agreement, acknowledgment, or as a filler in conversation, similar to "uh-huh" or "mmm" in English.

Gānbēi (干杯): A drinking toast in Chinese culture, translating to "dry the cup." It is a social expectation to finish one's drink in response.

Huángjiǔ (黄酒): Often translated as "Yellow Wine," this is a variety of Chinese fermented wine made from grains such as rice, with a sweet flavor profile.

Páo (袍,): A robe or gown worn since ancient times, typically by men. It is a long, loose-fitting outer garment with wide sleeves and a straight cut, made from materials like silk or cotton. The páo is both elegant and comfortable, symbolizing traditional Chinese attire.

Zhíjū (直裾): A straight-cut garment associated with formal or ceremonial occasions. It features a simple, vertical design and is often worn by scholars or officials. The zhíjū embodies modesty and propriety, reflecting ancient Chinese cultural values.

Rǔxiāng (乳香): Refers to the aroma of frankincense, traditionally believed to protect and purify. It is a popular scent for incense.

TERMS OF ENDEARMENT

Dìdì (弟弟): Means "Little Brother." This term is used to refer affectionately to a younger brother or a younger male.

Gēgē (哥哥): Translates to "Big Brother." Used for an older brother or a male elder in a respectful and affectionate manner.

Jiějie (姐姐): Translates to "Big Sister." Used to refer to an older sister or a female elder in a respectful and affectionate manner.

Mèimei (妹妹): Means "Little Sister." It is used affectionately for a younger sister or a younger female.

Nǎinai (奶奶): Grandma (paternal); can also be used respectfully for older women.

CULTURAL SYMBOLS & TRADITIONS

Concentrated Essence of Love: Historically, poets and scholars have referred to jade as the "Concentrated Essence of Love" due to its significance and value in Chinese culture. Jade is not only cherished for its beauty but also for its representation of purity, moral integrity, and protection. Its association with love comes from these qualities, along with the belief in its power to connect the spiritual and physical realms.

Double Happiness (囍 called "双喜" Shuāngxǐ): This symbol, composed of two adjacent Chinese characters for "happiness," is emblematic of joy and marital bliss. It is traditionally used in decorations for weddings and other celebrations to bring good luck and happiness to couples.

Double Seventh Festival (七夕节, Qīxī Jié): Celebrated on the seventh day of the seventh lunar month, this festival is often regarded as the Chinese Valentine's Day. It is rooted in the romantic legend of the Cowherd (牛郎, Niú Láng) and the Weaver Girl (织女, Zhī Nǚ), whose love was forbidden. Thus, they were banished to opposite sides of the Silver River (symbolizing the Milky Way) and allowed to meet just once a year on this day. The festival embodies themes of love, separation, and reunion.

Peony Flowers (牡丹, Mǔdān): Revered as "the King of Flowers," peonies symbolize wealth, prosperity, and honor in Chinese culture. They are also associated with feminine beauty, love, and affection. Traditionally, peonies are considered a good omen for happy marriages and fortune, making them a popular motif in art and celebrations.

Zhuazhou (抓周) is a traditional Chinese ceremony held on a child's first birthday, marking an important milestone. During the ceremony, various objects are placed in front of the child, such as a book, a brush, a coin, or a toy. The item the child selects is believed to indicate their future interests or career path. For example, choosing a book might suggest a future as a scholar, while picking up a coin could signify a future in finance or business. This custom reflects the hopes and aspirations parents have for their child's future and is a cherished cultural tradition celebrating the child's growth and potential.

CHARACTER NAMES

Yinuo(依诺 yī nuò);
Means: Follow, Promise.
Pronunciation: Yee-noo-oh.
Eldest Daughter.

Danbei (旦北 dàn běi);
Means: Dawn, North.
Pronunciation: Dan-bay.
Eldest Son.

Weixin (威心 wēi xīn);
Means: Majestic, Heart.
Pronunciation: Way-sheen.
Second Son.

Danni (旦尼 dàn ní);
Means: Dawn, Serenity.
Pronunciation: Dan-nee.
Third Son.

Ruijian (瑞健 ruì jiàn);
Means: Auspicious, Health.
Pronunciation: Roo-ay-jee-an.
Fourth Son.

Mingdan (明旦 míng dàn);
Means: Bright, Dawn.
Pronunciation: Ming-dan.
Fifth Son.

Sile (思乐 sī lè);
Means: Thought, Joy.

Pronunciation: Suh-luh.
Sixth Son.

Dehai (德海 dé hǎi);
Means: Virtue, Ocean.
Pronunciation: Duh-hai.
Gardener's Son, Servant to Yan.

Lord Nie (聂 niè):
Means: Whisper
Pronunciation: Nyeah.
Maternal Uncle & Adoptive Father of Cuilin

Cuilin (翠林 cuì lín);
Means: Jade Forest.
Pronunciation: Tsway-lin.
Prince of Zhou.

Lei Xing(雷星 léi xīng);
Means: Thunder, Star.
Pronunciation: Lay- sheeng.
Eldest Daughter of General Lei.

Lei Yingzhe (雷英哲 léi yīng zhé);
Means: Thunder, Hero, Wise.
Pronunciation: Lay-ying-jur.
Eldest Son of General Lei.

Yan (严 yán);
Means: Strict.
Pronunciation: Yan.
Family name of Yinuo.

Yaolin (瑶琳 yáo lín);
Means: Elegant Jade, Beautiful Forest.
Pronunciation: Yow-lin.
Madame Yan's personal maid.

Gao (高 gāo);
Means: High.
Pronunciation: Gow.
Madame Yan's eldest brother.

Taomei (桃美 táo měi);
Means: Peach, Beautiful.
Pronunciation: Tao-may.
Uncle Gao's daughter.